AARON RODD, DIVINER

AARON RODD, DIVINER

E. PHILLIPS OPPENHEIM

**INTRODUCTION
BY KARL WURF**

WILDSIDE PRESS

INTRODUCTION

KARL WURF

Edward Phillips Oppenheim (1866–1946) was one of the most prolific writers of popular fiction in the early 20th century. With more than 100 novels to his name, he played a formative role in shaping the modern thriller, particularly in the areas of espionage, international crime, and high-society intrigue. His books were widely read in Britain and America, and many remain in print today.

Oppenheim's fiction was defined by a mix of suspense, diplomacy, and glamour. His protagonists are often ordinary or disillusioned men—businessmen, lawyers, or minor government officials—who become entangled in dangerous plots involving theft, blackmail, or political betrayal. The tone is frequently ambiguous: criminals may become heroes, and law-abiding men may fall into moral gray zones. This thematic tension made his work both popular and influential in the development of crime and spy literature.

He was influenced by the Victorian sensation novel and the serial fiction model, but brought a distinctly modern sensibility to the structure and pacing of his stories. Unlike his predecessors, Oppenheim wrote with brisk economy and a sharp eye for psychological tension. He helped establish many of the genre conventions later seen in the work of authors like John Buchan, Eric Ambler, and even Ian Fleming.

Aaron Rodd, Diviner was first published in book form in 1919, following its earlier appearance as a serial in *Harper's Bazaar*. Though less widely known than Oppenheim's major thrillers, it stands out as a crime story that leans toward noir, centering on a morally compromised lawyer drawn into a jewel-smuggling plot. The novel offers a grittier, more psychological tone than many of his earlier works.

This edition reintroduces a work of fiction that reflects both its time and a timeless fascination with crime, conscience, and survival. Oppenheim remains a key figure in the history of suspense fiction, and this novel adds nuance to his legacy.

For further reading, those new to Oppenheim might consider starting with *The Great Impersonation*, his best-known novel of espionage and identity deception. Also notable are *The Malefactor*, a story of revenge and redemption; *The Spy Paramount*, which immerses readers in the world of covert politics; and *The Double Traitor*, a spy novel rich in political detail. His stories often feature European settings, aristocratic villains, and complex female characters, all wrapped in a crisp, accessible prose style.

CHAPTER I

THE CUNNING OF HARVEY GRIMM

A queer, unexpected streak of sunshine, which by some miracle had found its way through a pall of clouds and low-hanging mist, suddenly fell as though exhausted across the asphalt path of the Embankment Gardens. A tall, gaunt young man, who had been seated with folded arms in the corner of one of the seats, stared at it as though bewildered. His eyes suddenly met those of a young lady in deep black, who was gazing about her in similar stupefaction. Almost at once, and with perfect spontaneity, she smiled upon him.

"But it is astonishing, this!" she exclaimed, "Sunshine in London—in January!"

The young man was a little confused. He was very diffident, and such lack of conventionality on the part of a perfect stranger surprised him.

"It is unusual," he admitted.

"It is a thing which I have never seen before," she went on, dropping her voice a little and glancing towards a bath-chair close at hand, in which an elderly and very delicate-looking old gentleman was muffled up in furs and apparently asleep. "It is something, even, for which I had not dared to hope. We seem so far here from everything that is bright and beautiful and cheerful."

Aaron Rodd, who was a shy and awkward being, felt unexpectedly at his ease. He was even anxious for further conversation. He had a rather long, pale face, with deep-set eyes and rugged features. He was soberly, even sombrely dressed in dismal black. He had the air of a recluse. Perhaps that was why the young lady smiled upon him with such confidence.

"You are not English?" he ventured. She shook her head.

"What we are now, alas!" she sighed, glancing towards the bath-chair. "I scarcely know, for we have no country. Like every one else in such a plight, we come to England."

"It is your father who sleeps there?" he inquired.

"It is my grandfather," she told him. "Together—he and I and my brother—we have passed through terrible times. He has lost all power to sleep at night. In the daytime, when it does not rain, he is wheeled out here, and only, if it is not too cold, then he sleeps as he does now, and I watch."

"You are very young to have charge of him."

She smiled a little pitifully. "One grows old so quickly in these terrible days! I am already twenty-one. But you," she went on—"see how inquisitive I am!—I saw you yesterday from the distance, seated here. There are nurse-maids and queer fragments of humanity who seem to pass through these gardens and loiter, and sometimes there are those with affairs who go on their way. But you—what do you think of as you sit there? You are a writer, perhaps?"

He laughed a little harshly. His voice was not altogether pleasant.

"I am a lawyer," he declared, "without a practice. Sometimes the ghosts who call at my empty office stifle me, and I come out here to escape from them."

"A lawyer? An *avocat*?" she repeated softly to herself.

Evidently she found something to interest her in the statement. She glanced towards the sleeping man. Then she came a little nearer. He was conscious of a very delightful and altogether un-English perfume, aware suddenly that her eyes were the colour of violets, framed underneath with deep but not unbecoming lines, that her mouth was curved in a fashion strange to him.

"Englishmen, they say, are so much to be trusted," she murmured, "and a lawyer too...."

"I am an American by birth," he interposed, "although I have lived over here nearly all my life."

"It is the same thing. We need advice so badly. Let me ask you one question. Is it not the first principle of a lawyer to hold sacred whatever confidence his client may confide in him?"

"Absolutely," he assured her.

"Even if that confidence," she persisted, "should bring the person who offered it within the hold of the law?"

"A lawyer may refuse a client," he said, "but he may never betray his confidence."

"Will you tell me your name and address?" she asked eagerly.

"My name is Aaron Rodd," he told her. "My address is number 17 Manchester Street, Adelphi, and my office is on the third floor."

"Mr. Aaron Rodd," she repeated, with a queer little foreign intonation. "That is a strange name and I shall remember it. When might one visit you, monsieur? At three o'clock this afternoon?"

"I shall be in all day."

"Then *au revoir*!" she exclaimed, with an abrupt gesture of farewell.

The old gentleman had opened his eyes and was gazing fretfully about. She crossed the asphalt walk swiftly towards him. An attendant, who seemed to have gone to sleep standing on one leg, gripped the handle of the bath-chair. The girl passed her arm around the old man's shoulders and whispered something to the attendant. They passed away together. The little streak of sunshine had gone. Aaron Rodd thrust his ungloved hands into his coat pockets and made his way in the opposite direction.

* * * *

About an hour later a small, rubicund man, a man whose dark hair was turning grey, but whose eyes were bright and whose complexion was remarkably healthy, paused before the door-plate of an office building in one of the back streets leading from the Adelphi. He was dressed with extreme neatness, from the tips of his patent boots to his grey felt hat, and he was obviously of a cheerful disposition. He glanced down the list of names, twirling his cane in light-hearted fashion and whistling softly to himself. Suddenly he paused. His cane ceased its aimless configurations and rested for a moment upon a name about half-way down the list, the name of Mr. Aaron Rodd, Solicitor and Commissioner for Oaths. There was also an indication that Mr. Rodd's offices were to be found upon the third floor. His prospective visitor glanced around, and, discovering that there was no lift, started out for the stone stairs. On the first landing he encountered a small boy, descending with a roll of papers under his arm. Him the newcomer, whose name was Mr. Harvey Grimm, promptly addressed.

"My young sir," he said pleasantly, "from the red tape around that bundle of papers which you are carrying. I gather that you have legal connections. You are probably the confidential clerk of the gentleman whom I am proposing to visit. Can you tell me, before I attempt another flight of these very dusty and unsympathetic steps, whether Mr. Aaron Rodd is within?"

The boy glanced at his questioner suspiciously.

"I am not in Mr. Rodd's office," he replied. "I'm Steel & Agnett, second floor."

"That," Mr. Harvey Grimm sighed regretfully, "is unfortunate. A very excellent firm yours, my boy. Do not let me any longer interfere with your efforts on their behalf."

Aaron Rodd's prospective visitor, with a sigh, recommenced the ascent. The boy looked after him for a moment dubiously and then disappeared. Arrived at the third floor, at the extreme end of the corridor the former discovered a door, on which was painted the name of *Mr. Aaron Rodd*. He knocked, was bidden to enter, and stepped at once into a single bald and unpromising-looking apartment.

"Good morning. Aaron!" he said cheerfully, closing the door behind him and advancing across the dusty floor.

Aaron Rodd, who had been seated before a desk, apparently immersed in a legal document, first raised his head and then rose slowly to his feet. His first look of expectancy, as he had turned towards his visitor, faded by degrees into a very curious expression, an expression which seemed made up of a great deal of amazement and a certain amount of dread. With his left hand he gripped the side of the desk.

"My God!" he exclaimed. "It's Ned—"

His visitor held out his hand.

"No, no, my dear Aaron," he interrupted firmly, "you are deceived by a slight resemblance. You are thinking, probably, of that poor fellow Ned Stiles. You will never see Ned again, Aaron."

The intelligence appeared to cause the listener no grief. Neither did it carry with it any conviction.

"Harvey Grimm is my name," the newcomer went on, "Mr. Harvey Grimm, if you please, of Chicago. You remember me now, without a doubt?"

He extended his hand confidently. His smile was ingratiating, his air that of an ingenuous child, anxious for a favourable reception. Aaron Rodd slowly thrust out his ink-stained fingers.

"I remember you all right," he admitted.

The visitor, having established his identity, seemed disposed to abandon the subject. He glanced around the room, and, discovering a cane-bottomed chair on which were piled some dust-covered documents, he calmly swept them away, annexed the chair, which he carefully flicked around with a silk handkerchief, and brought it to the side of the desk.

"Sit down, my dear fellow. I beg you," he invited, laying his hat on the floor by his side, hitching up his blue serge trousers and smiling in momentary satisfaction at his well-polished shoes.

"I have appropriated. I fancy, the clients' chair. Am I right, I wonder, in presuming that there has not been much use for it lately?"

"Perfectly right," was the grim reply.

"Hard times these have been for all of us," Harvey Grimm declared, with an air of placid satisfaction. "You are not expecting a client this morning, I presume?"

"Nor a miracle."

"In that case I will smoke," the newcomer continued, producing a small gold case, selecting a cigarette, and lighting it. "Try one."

Aaron Rodd hesitated, and finally accepted the offer. He smoked with the air of one unused to the indulgence.

"Mr. Harvey Grimm of Chicago," he muttered, studying his visitor's very immaculate appearance. "Haven't I heard the name somewhere, or seen it in the papers lately?"

"Possibly," was the suave reply. "My arrival in London has, I think, created some slight interest. Even your Press, I find, is not above recording the movements of a capitalist."

"A what?"

"A capitalist," Harvey Grimm repeated calmly. "With a name like mine, and an abode like Chicago, I am amazed that you did not divine it."

"Seven years ago," Aaron Rodd observed, "we divided seventeen pounds four shillings and eight pence. It was, I believe, our united capital."

"And to judge by your surroundings," his companion sighed, "I fear, my friend, that you have been emulating the man who tied up his talent in a stocking. I, on the other hand——"

"Have changed your name and become a capitalist," Aaron Rodd interrupted drily.

"Precisely!"

There was a moment's silence. Mr. Harvey Grimm, with the beatific smile of opulence, was whistling softly to himself. His companion's thoughts had apparently travelled back into the past.

"Well," the latter said at last, "I will imitate your candour. The document I was examining with so much interest when you came in is a seven-year old lease, long since cancelled. The few black boxes you see around the room are, with one exception, bogus. I sit here from morning till night and nothing happens. I sit here and brood."

"Dear me!—dear me!" his visitor murmured sympathetically.

"By turning my chair around," Aaron Rodd continued. "I can just catch a glimpse of the river across the gardens there. I sit and watch—wonder whether a tug will go past next or a lighter; watch the people in the gardens—wonder where they are going, why they are loitering, why hurrying. I speculate about the few passers-by down in the street there. Sometimes I close my eyes and I fancy myself in Lincoln's Inn, seated in a padded morocco chair, with a Turkey-carpet on the floor, and rows of boxes, black tin boxes, with wonderful names inscribed upon them in white lettering, reaching to the ceiling, and my secretary poring over my engagement book, wondering when it would be possible for me to squeeze in half an hour for an important client."

"Too much of the dreamer about you," Harvey Grimm pronounced. "Perhaps, after all, it is the fault of your work. It's a sedative profession, you know, Aaron. It wouldn't suit me to have to sit and wait for clients."

"It's the black bogey of my life," the other assented, with a thin note of passion in his tone. "If only one could get out and work, even if one didn't get a penny for it!"

"And financially?" Harvey Grimm inquired, with an apologetic cough.

"On the rocks," was the bitter reply. "You can understand," he went on, with a heedless sarcasm, "what a wonderful thing it is for me to welcome a capitalist in my shabby office."

"And an old friend," was the cheerful reminder. "Come, come, Aaron, we must look into this. I must place some of my affairs in your charge."

Aaron Rodd's lip curled with bitter incredulity. "Some of your affairs! I had a taste of those in the old days. Ned—I mean Harvey. You brought me to the brink of Sing-Sing; you drove me over here to make a fresh start."

Harvey Grimm waved his hand. These reminiscences were indelicate.

"My dear fellow!" he protested. "Now come, answer me a few questions. Such affairs of business as have fallen to your lot have been conducted with—er—discretion?"

"If you mean have I preserved my reputation," the lawyer replied grimly, "I have. I have had no temptation to do otherwise."

"That is capital," his friend declared. "That helps us at once. And now, I think," he went on, glancing at his neat little wristwatch, "—lunch."

Aaron Rodd's first movement was almost eager. He checked himself, however. Then a glance at his visitor's immaculate toilet and distinctly opulent appearance reassured him.

"There will be no trouble. I presume," he said a little diffidently, "as to the settlement of our bill? I warn you before we start that a shilling and a few coppers—"

Harvey Grimm laid his hand almost affectionately upon the other's shoulder.

"My dear Aaron," he expostulated, "you are a little confused. You have not yet taken in the position. A capitalist is, of course, a relative term. I will not press that point. But let me assure you that I have a suite of rooms at the Milan, ample credit for any meals I choose to take there, even money to pay for them, if necessary."

"I am not fit to go to the Milan," Aaron Rodd muttered, brushing himself vigorously.

"That is entirely your mistake," his friend replied, rising to his feet and lighting another cigarette. "A judicious shabbiness is today an approved form of eccentricity. With your ascetic face, my dear Aaron, that little wisp of black tie, your clean but frayed collar, your sombre, well-worn clothes, you would be mistaken by the casual observer for either a Chancery lawyer with an indifferent housekeeper, or a writer of dramatic blank verse, which every one admires but no one buys. Reassure yourself, Aaron. I predict that as a companion you will do me every credit."

For the first time a grim, hard smile parted the lips of the man who was making out with rather weary fingers the accustomed card to affix to his door.

"The needy adventurer is what I feel like in these days," he observed.

"And why not adventurer?" Harvey Grimm protested, as they descended the stone steps. "We are all needy, that is to say we all need something or other, and we all—those of us who understand life, at any rate—seek adventures. Even with the success I have myself attained—I will be quite frank with you, my dear Aaron—I am entirely unchanged. I can assure you that I am not above finding interest and pleasure, as well as profit, in any adventure which may come to hand."

His companion chuckled drily.

"I can well believe it," he murmured.

They strolled up the street, a somewhat curiously assorted couple. Mr. Harvey Grimm's grey felt hat, his neat and somewhat jaunty figure, rather suggested the successful trainer of careful habits, or elderly jockey enjoying the opulence of middle-age. Aaron Rodd, on the other hand, looked exactly what he was—the lean and hungry professional man with whom the times have gone ill.

"Queer neighbourhood, this you've chosen for your office, Aaron," his friend remarked, pausing as they neared the corner. "What sort of people come into these parts, anyway?"

"It's just a backwater. There's the broad stream of London flowing on to success and prosperity a few yards up the hill. If you listen for a moment, you can hear it. These little streets are just parasitical branches, still alive and still struggling, but fit for nothing but to be snapped off. All the furtive businesses in the world might be conducted behind these silent, unwashed windows and blank doorways—shabby theatrical agencies, doubtful publications, betting offices of poor reputation. People come here to hide or to escape notice. There was a murder committed down by the railings at the end of the street, only a year or so ago."

"Obviously," Harvey Grimm remarked cheerfully, "the region of melancholia and tragedies. We must see how things go, Aaron. Perhaps, later on, it would be as well for you to move to a better-known part. Just at present, however, it is well enough."

The tall young man looked down at his companion half derisively, half eagerly. He knew him too well to ask many questions, knew him too well to hope unduly, knew, too, the danger into which this simple luncheon might lead him. Yet only a few nights ago he had thought of the river! It was better to take luncheon with Harvey Grimm at the Milan than to feel the black waters sucking his breath away!

* * * *

"Feeling better. Aaron?" Harvey Grimm inquired of his friend, about an hour and a half later.

Aaron Rodd was both feeling and looking better, and acknowledged the fact. His manner towards his host, too, showed signs of a subtle change. The latter was obviously *persona grata* in the restaurant. Their table, although a little retired, was in a coveted corner, and attentions of every sort had been respectfully offered them. Nevertheless, his guest felt some sense of relief when he saw the bill signed with a little flourish and accepted with a low bow by their waiter. Harvey Grimm leaned back in his chair and removed the cigar for a moment from his lips.

"You've no faith in me, Aaron," he declared, with an encouraging smile; "that's what you always lacked, even in the old days—faith. You're losing touch with the world, you know, cooped up in that musty office of yours. You don't expect anything to happen to you so long as you grub away there, do you?"

"Nothing has happened, at any rate," Aaron Rodd admitted.

"I will not say that it is your fault," his companion continued tolerantly. "You are by nature of a meditative and retiring temperament. It is a piece of extraordinarily good fortune for you that I never forget old friends."

"Have you anything to propose to me?" Aaron Rodd asked bluntly.

His host leaned across the table. "Always so downright, my dear Aaron," he murmured, "so material! However, you have asked the question and here is my answer. I am proposing to remain in London for some little time. There are various schemes which have suggested themselves to me, which might readily lead to an enlargement of my income. For their prosecution, my dear Aaron, I need one, only one companion whom I can trust, one man who is out for the big things. That is why I come to you. I offer you a partnership in the concern—Harvey Grimm & Rodd, Traffickers in Fate, Dealers in Adventures.... How your hand shakes, man! There, you've dropped the ash from your cigar!"

Aaron Rodd's thin lips were quivering. His eyes seemed full of unutterable things.

"I have made such a fight of it," he muttered. "You've got me though, Harvey. I've eaten my last crust. I should have had to sell my office stool for a meal tomorrow."

His friend shook his head genially. "My dear Aaron," he protested, "such a confession from a man of brains, when one considers how the world is overrun with fools, is a terrible one."

"One has a conscience," Rodd sighed, "and a profession like mine doesn't lend itself to crooked dealing."

Harvey Grimm smiled tolerantly. He had the air of one listening to a child.

"The wolves of the world," he said, "keep their conscience, and as regards wrong-doing, it's just success that makes the difference.... My dear fellow!" he broke off, looking up into the face of a man who had paused at their table and whose hand was now reposing heavily upon his shoulder. "My dear Brodie, this is most opportune. Let me present you to my friend Mr. Aaron Rodd. Aaron, this is Mr. Brodie—in the language of the cinemas," he added, dropping his voice a little and leaning forward, "the sleuth-hound of Europe, the greatest living detective."

Aaron Rodd sat for a moment motionless. The cigar slipped from his fingers onto the plate. All his new hopes seemed crumbling away. His eyes were fixed upon the hand which gripped his companion's shoulder. Harvey Grimm began to laugh softly.

"Cheer up, my pessimistic friend!" he exclaimed. "This isn't the grip of the law which is upon my shoulder. Mr. Brodie and I are friends—I might even say allies."

Aaron Rodd recovered himself and murmured a few words of mechanical greeting. The newcomer meanwhile took the chair which the waiter had offered him. He was a tall, burly man, clean-shaven, with steely grey eyes, and grey hair brushed back from his forehead. His manner was consequential, his tone patronising. "So this is our third hand, eh?"

"Guessed it in one with your usual astuteness," Harvey Grimm acknowledged cheerfully. "A lawyer of unblemished character, not momentarily affluent, with the principles of a latitudinarian."

"Has he got the nerve?" Mr. Brodie demanded. "If we are on the right track, there's no room for weaklings in the job."

"Aaron Rodd's all right," his friend declared confidently. "You leave that to me. I'll answer for him."

The younger man leaned across the table.

"Do I understand," he inquired, "that our enterprise is on the side of the law?"

Harvey Grimm smiled.

"The present one, my dear Aaron. I should explain to you, perhaps, that Mr. Brodie is not officially attached either to Scotland Yard or to Police Headquarters in New York. He spent some years at Scotland Yard, and, having the good-luck to inherit a small fortune, and feeling himself handicapped by the antiquated methods and jealousies of his competitors, he decided to strike out for himself as an independent investigator. Some day he will tell us a few of his adventures."

Mr. Brodie had folded his arms and was looking very imposing.

"I have hunted criminals," he asserted, "in every quarter of the world. I have methods of my own. I have a genius for making use of people."

"So you see, my dear Aaron," Harvey Grimm pointed out, "at present Mr. Brodie and I are the greatest of friends. He recognises the fact that I am what is baldly spoken of as an adventurer, and that the time may come when we shall find ourselves in opposite camps, but just at present it is our privilege to be of service to Mr. Brodie."

Then a thing, ordinary enough in its way, happened in a curious manner. Mr. Brodie was a large man, but he seemed suddenly to fade away. There was his empty chair and a dim vision of a retreating figure behind one of the central sideboards. Aaron Rodd seemed dimly conscious of a look of warning flashed between the two men, but nothing equal to the swift secrecy of Mr. Brodie's movements had ever confused his senses. Harvey Grimm leaned across the table, holding his liqueur glass in his hand.

"Slick fellow. Brodie," he murmured. "No good his being seen talking to us when the quarry's about, eh? Nice brandy, this. On the dry side, perhaps, but with a flavour to it."

Aaron Rodd understood that he was to ask no questions, and he discussed the subject of brandy in a sufficiently ignorant manner. He, too, however, within the course of the next few seconds, found need for the exercise of all his powers of self-control. Only a few yards away from him was a young man in some foreign uniform, with his arm in a sling, discussing with a *maître d'hôtel* as to the locality of his table. By his side was the girl with whom he had talked that morning in the Embankment Gardens, and behind the two, a somewhat pathetic picture, was the old man, his face as withered as parchment, his narrow white beard carefully trimmed, leaning heavily upon a stick. Almost as he realised their presence they moved on, escorted by the *maître d'hôtel* to a table in a distant corner. Aaron Rodd drew a long breath as they disappeared. His companion looked at him curiously.

"Are those the people," the lawyer asked eagerly, "on whose account Brodie moved away?"

Harvey Grimm watched them settle in their places.

"They are," he admitted. "A pathetic-looking trio! ... And now, my dear Aaron," he went on, "we will discuss your little adventure in the Embankment Gardens this morning. You perceive that the moment is appropriate."

"My little adventure?" Aaron Rodd repeated blankly. "Why—you mean to say you were there, then? You saw her speak to me?"

"Certainly! I was seated a little further down, talking with my friend Mr. Brodie. We had our eyes upon the young lady."

Aaron Rodd felt a sudden disinclination to speak of that little gleam of sunshine.

"She spoke to me quite casually," he declared. "Afterwards she asked me my profession. I told her that I was a lawyer. Perhaps she had already guessed it. I suppose I do rather look the part."

"You do indeed, my friend! And then?"

The younger man hesitated. His partner's benevolent face suddenly assumed a sterner aspect.

"Aaron," he reminded him, "we are on business. The truth, please—no reservations."

"She asked me," the other went on, "whether the confidence of a client is always respected by one in my profession."

"And your reply?"

"I assured her, of course, that under any circumstances it was."

Harvey Grimm leaned back in his chair. He rolled the remaining drop of brandy around in his glass: his expression was beatific.

"My dear Aaron," he said, "fate smiles upon our new partnership. The young lady is going to pay you a visit?"

"At three o'clock this afternoon, if she keeps her word."

"Finish your brandy and come with me to my apartment," Harvey Grimm directed. "We have matters to discuss and arrange before you receive that visit."

* * * *

An hour or so later. Aaron Rodd was seated once more before his dilapidated, ink-stained desk. The gloom of the winter afternoon was only partly dissipated by the single gas-jet burning above his head. The same old lease was spread out underneath his hands. In his face, however, there was a distinct change. The listlessness had gone. He had the air of one awaiting events. So he had sat for the last half-hour, with his eyes fixed alternately upon the outside door, purposely left ajar, and the inner one which led to his humble bed-sitting room.

There came at last the sound for which he had been waiting. Up that last flight of stone stairs he could hear distinctly the slow movement of weary footsteps, the continual tapping of a stick, the occasional cough and querulous complaint of a tired old man, and by the side of those shuffling footsteps, others, marvellously light, the swish of a silken skirt, the music of a clear, very sweet young voice.

"You see, we are arrived," she was saying. "There is the name upon the door. You will be able to sit down directly. Courage, dear grandfather. Remember, it is for Leopold's sake."

Then there followed a gentle knock, the somewhat hesitating entrance of the two, the half-doubtful look of the girl towards the tall, gaunt young man whose face seemed almost saturnine underneath that unshaded light. As he moved forward, however, she recognised him, and a smile of relief parted her lips.

"Ah! it is Mr. Rodd, is it not—the gentleman with whom I spoke in the Gardens this morning—the lawyer?"

He bowed. Anxiety made his voice sound even harsher. Many things had happened since the morning.

"You have kept your promise, then," he remarked. "You have come to consult me. I am at your service. One moment."

He brought two of the chairs which stood stiffly against the wall, and placed them by the side of his desk. The old man sat down with an air of relief. The passage up the stairs had apparently exhausted him.

"We are very haphazard clients, I fear, Mr. Rodd," he said wearily. "This is unfortunately one of my bad days. I must leave my granddaughter to explain the reason of our visit, and in what manner we hope to be able to make use of your services."

"If I do so, grandfather," she said, turning a little towards him, "I am going to tell the whole truth."

"If it must be," he murmured uneasily. The girl took up at once the burden of explanation.

"My grandfather, my brother, and myself," she began, "are staying at the Milan Hotel. We make use of a name, the name of Brinnen, to which we have some right, even though it may be a shadowy one. We happen to be Belgians by birth, a fact which at the present moment makes our position easier. To be honest with you, however, my brother has just returned from America. He has been engaged for some time in more hazardous enterprises, even, than defending his country against the Germans."

The old man interrupted her impatiently.

"These explanations are waste of time," he insisted. "Tell this gentleman quickly what we desire of him."

She patted his hand and glanced half-apologetically across at Aaron Rodd. He had resumed his seat before his desk, his face half-hidden by his hand. Listening to the girl's voice, he had become conscious of a long-forgotten sentiment. Encumbered though she was with a difficult mission, there was a certain fineness of speech and manner, an appeal for sympathy even in this last gesture, which he found strangely disturbing.

"You need explain to me no more than you wish," he told her, a little Stiffly. "I shall be glad to be of any service to you. There is no need for you to enter into any painful details."

She shrugged her shoulders protestingly.

"You and my grandfather are of one mind," she remarked. "Then I will make a confession which may sound abrupt, but which is nevertheless true. We three—my brother, my grandfather, and myself—are not entitled to the sympathy we receive. We are, to a certain extent, impostors. Is your standard of morals a very high one, Mr. Rodd?"

"I—I scarcely really know," he stammered. "As a lawyer I am brought into contact with all conditions of people. I have before now done my best for the criminal as I have for the honest man."

"It is reassuring," she admitted. "Behold, then, my full confession. You have to do now with criminals—or may I say adventurers? We have, we three, to dispose of secretly a very large amount of precious stones. I have come to you for advice. The ordinary avenues of sale are closed to us. How can we get into touch with someone who will buy them and ask no questions?"

Aaron Rodd was conscious of a little shock. Up to this last moment he had been doubtful. Notwithstanding the story which had been unfolded to him by Harvey Grimm, he had clung to his first impressions—impressions from which he was parting now with dire reluctance.

"It is not an easy matter," he admitted, "but if anyone can help you, I can." The girl nodded.

"There must be secrecy," she declared. "You see, my brother is, in a way, notorious. He has been very daring and very successful. For the sake of those who buy them, as well as our own sake, the jewels must not be recognised afterwards."

"I have a friend who might arrange it," Aaron Rodd announced. "I must warn you, however, that selling your stones in this way you cannot possibly receive their full value."

"We do not expect that," old man mumbled. "What we want, though, is the money—quickly."

"My friend could doubtless manage that," the lawyer declared.

"When can we see him?" the girl asked eagerly.

"At once," was the prompt reply. "He was with me when you came, and I sent him into my private apartments. If it is your wish, I will fetch him."

"By all means," the old man insisted eagerly.

"Yes, yes!" the girl echoed.

Aaron Rodd rose to his feet and crossed the room to the door which led into his private apartment. He opened it, and beckoned to its unseen occupant.

"I have some clients here who would like a word with you, Grimm," he announced. "There may, perhaps, be some business."

Harvey Grimm made his appearance at once. His air of curiosity, as he looked into the room, was very well done.

"Business?" he repeated.

"This gentleman and young lady," Aaron Rodd explained, "are clients of mine. Their names are unnecessary. They have consulted me as to the disposal of valuable jewels, their claim to which—might be open to question."

Harvey Grimm threw the cigar which he had been smoking into the fireplace.

"I see," he murmured. "Better tell me the circumstances."

The girl repeated her story, with a few more details. The old man listened in a sort of placid stupor. He interrupted only once.

"It is a foolish way, this. There is a man in Amsterdam—"

"You will tell me what you advise, monsieur," the girl begged. "We must have money, and the jewels must be made unrecognisable."

Harvey Grimm took a small magnifying glass from his pocket and screwed it together.

"You have probably brought some of the stones with you," he observed briskly.

The girl hesitated. She turned to her companion as though for guidance. He was still mumbling to himself, however, something about Amsterdam.

"It is absolutely essential," Harvey Grimm continued, "that I should know something definite about the character of the stones you have to offer—that is if you wish me to deal with them."

There was a brief silence. Then the girl rose to her feet and deliberately turned away from the three men for several moments. When she swung around again, she held in her hand a small chamois leather bag. Very carefully she opened it and shook out its contents into the palm of Harvey Grimm's outstretched hand.

"The large one," she said simply, "belonged to an American millionaire. My brother says that it is worth twenty thousand pounds. He, too, is a wonderful judge of precious stones."

The old man seemed to wake up for a moment.

"It is worth," he faltered, "a king's ransom."

They all three bent over the little collection of jewels. Aaron Rodd's expression was one of simple curiosity. His knowledge of diamonds was nil. His partner's manner, on the other hand, underwent a curious change. There was a hard glitter in his eyes and unsuspected lines about his mouth. The atmosphere of the little room had become charged with new forces. The girl's face was tense with excitement, the old man seemed suddenly and subtly different.

"Do not waste time," the former begged, a little feverishly. "It is not safe to bring these jewels into the daylight, even here. If you will buy, state your price. Give us an idea. We can meet again, perhaps."

Harvey Grimm turned towards them. "The small stones are negligible," he pronounced. "The large stone is worth quite as much as you say. To cut it up, however, and then to sell it in a secret market, is another thing. The most you could hope for would be five thousand pounds."

The girl's face was a little vague. "Tell me," she inquired, "in English money how much is that a year?"

"Two hundred and fifty pounds."

"So that if there were ten stones like that," she went on, a little wistfully, "that would be an income of two thousand, two hundred and fifty pounds. One would live comfortably on that? One could hide somewhere in a quiet country place and live like gentlefolk—"

"Certainly," Harvey Grimm assured her. She turned a little doubtfully towards her companion.

"I am afraid," she sighed, "that grandfather is almost past realising what money means. In any case, we must consult my brother."

Then there came without warning an interruption which seemed equally startling to all of them. Without any preliminary summons, the door of the office was thrown open. The detective, Brodie, followed by a man in plain clothes, but with an unmistakably professional appearance, entered the room. The latter closed the door behind him. Brodie approached the little group. The girl's eyes were lit with terror. Harvey Grimm dropped his handkerchief over the jewels, whilst his partner stepped forward. Aaron Rodd's tone was harsh with anxiety, his face seemed more drawn than ever.

"What do you want here?" he demanded. Mr. Brodie smiled tolerantly. His eyes were fixed upon the table. He pushed the questioner on one side and lifted the handkerchief which Harvey Grimm had thrown over the diamonds. Then he turned towards his companion with a little cry of triumph.

"That," he declared, pointing to the jewel upon the table, "is one of the Van Hutten diamonds."

"I do not understand," the girl said quietly enough, although she was shaking from head to foot. "It belongs to us. It is the property of—"

"Cut it out," Brodie interrupted brusquely. "We'll talk to you young lady, at police headquarters."

The girl turned to Aaron Rodd.

"Who is this man, and what does he want?" she cried. "Is this a trap into which you have drawn us? Is it a crime, here in England, then, to offer jewels for sale?"

"We'll talk this all out at the police station," Brodie intervened curtly. "Inspector?"

The man in plain clothes stepped forward and took command of the situation.

"My instructions are," he announced politely, "to ask you both to come with me to the police-station."

The old gentleman simply looked dazed. He rose to his feet obediently and turned towards the girl. She patted his arm reassuringly, but there was a look in her face which brought a sob into Aaron Rodd's throat. He was filled all the time with a silent fury. He cursed the moment which had taken him into the Embankment Gardens, which had brought Harvey Grimm once more into his life. The single look which the girl had flashed upon him was like a dagger in his heart.

Brodie had replaced the diamonds, one by one, in the little bag. He handed them over to his companion, and motioned them all towards the door. The old gentleman moved wearily along, leaning upon his granddaughter's arm. Aaron Rodd hurried forward and opened the door. He tried to say something, but the girl turned from him contemptuously. He stood on the threshold, listening to their slow footsteps as they descended into the street. Then he swung back into the room, slammed the door, and sank into the chair in front of his desk. It was as though he had passed through some terrible nightmare. He sat gazing out through the shadows. Had it all really happened? Then he caught a faint, unfamiliar breath of perfume which suddenly set his heart beating with unaccustomed vigour. A little morsel of white lace lay underneath the chair upon which she had been seated. He stooped and picked it up, smoothed it out, and let it slip from his lingers almost in despair. It was all true, then! She had sat in that chair, had come to his office, trusting him, had walked into the Harvey-Grimm-cum-Brodie trap!

It was an hour or more before Harvey Grimm returned. He closed the door after him and came briskly across the floor.

"Well, young fellow," he exclaimed, "you can't say that I haven't fished you out of the backwaters."

"I wish to God you'd left me there!" was the bitter reply. "Tell me what's happened to her?"

"To her?—oh—the young lady," Harvey Grimm murmured, with an illuminating smile. "She's all right. She's back at the Milan by this time."

"They couldn't identify the diamond, then?" Aaron Rodd asked eagerly.

"Not by a long chalk," was the smiling reply. "To tell you the truth. Brodie's about the sickest man in London just now. The stone he rolled out in front of the expert they had waiting down at Scotland Yard was—"

"Was what?"

"A lump of paste," Harvey Grimm declared, lighting a cigarette. "Queer business, eh?"

"There's no charge against the old gentleman and his granddaughter, then?" Aaron Rodd demanded breathlessly.

"None whatever. Why not try a cigarette, Aaron? You're all nerves."

The lawyer pushed the box away from him.

"You may think this sort of thing's worth while," he declared gloomily. "I can't say that I do. There'll be no reward to share, and it seems to me that we've made an enemy—"

"There's no reward," Harvey Grimm agreed, "but there's this."

He drew his handkerchief from his pocket. A diamond almost as large as a cob-nut rolled over and lay upon the desk. Aaron Rodd stared at it in amazement.

"What's that?" he demanded.

"One of the Van Hutten diamonds," was the triumphant reply. "Look at it well. You won't see it again. By this time tomorrow it will have been cut."

Aaron Rodd was stupefied. He looked from the stone up to his companion's face. Even his demand for some elucidation was mute.

"I had the duplicate ready," Harvey Grimm explained. "That was my game. I changed them underneath my handkerchief. It was perfectly easy. They've got the imitation one at police headquarters and they aren't feeling particularly pleased with themselves. That fellow Brodie is about the bummest detective who ever crossed the Atlantic."

Aaron Rodd was sitting transfixed. His fingers were shaking as they beat upon the desk.

"My God," he exclaimed, as light streamed in upon him, "we're thieves!"

"Don't talk like a fool," the other admonished. "It's a fair enough game between crooks. We've stolen a stolen jewel, and by doing it we've saved the girl and her grandfather and her brother, too, from gaol. That's fair, isn't it? When I've finished with that, there'll be a matter of three or four thousand pounds for us to divide. What about it, eh?"

He swept the jewel back into his pocket. Aaron Rodd's fingers were still idly beating upon the desk. The walls of his dusty, bare apartment had fallen away, the thrall of his sordid poverty lay no longer like a dead-weight upon his spirits. Three or four thousand pounds to divide!

"What you need," Harvey Grimm declared briskly, handing him his hat, "is a drink. Come right along."

CHAPTER II

POETRY BY COMPULSION

Mr. Paul Brodie walked, unannounced, into Aaron Rodd's office, a matter of ten days after the episode of the changed diamond. He had lost a little of his bombast, and he carried himself with less than his usual confidence. His eyes, however, had lost none of their old inquisitive fire. He was perfectly well aware, even as he greeted the two men who rose to welcome him, that Aaron Rodd was wearing a new suit of clothes, that the office had been spring-cleaned, that the box of cigarettes upon the desk were of an expensive brand, and that the violets in the buttonhole of Harvey Grimm's immaculate coat had come from a Bond Street florist.

"Good morning, gentlemen," he said airily, subsiding into the chair which the latter had vacated for him. "Nice little trio of conspirators we are, eh?"

Harvey Grimm shrugged his shoulders.

"It's rough on you," he admitted—"gives you kind of a twist, of course, with the police—but I can't see any sense in the thing yet. They weren't meaning to trade off that bit of paste on a diamond expert surely!"

The detective scratched his chin.

"That bit of paste," he declared, "was all they had on them, any way. Seems as though they hadn't quite sized you up—you and Mr. Rodd here—and were paying you a test visit. Gee, they're clever!"

"You had them searched, I suppose," the other inquired, "to be sure they hadn't the real goods with them?"

"You bet!" the detective assented gloomily. "Made it all the worse for us afterwards. I tell you I daren't show my face at Scotland Yard these days."

Harvey Grimm nodded sympathetically.

"Still, they must know that these people aren't what they profess to be," he observed.

"That's all very well," Brodie agreed, "but everyone goes about with kid gloves on in this country. That's why I threw up my job and went over to the States. Even a criminal, a known criminal, has got to be treated as though he were a little God Almighty until the charge is right there and the proof lying handy. I spent last night with Inspector Ditchwater. He's as sure as I am that the young man is no other than Jeremiah Sands, but he'd sooner let him slip through his fingers than take a risk."

"How does it come about, then," Aaron Rodd asked quietly, "that a famous diamond thief is wearing the uniform of a Belgian officer, that he is decorated and wounded?"

"Simple as possible," Brodie explained. "We knew perfectly well that Jeremiah Sands was a Belgian. That little fact has been in every description of him that's ever been issued. He chucked his little enterprises in New York, the moment war was declared, and sailed for Europe, bringing the loot with him. He was as clever as paint, though. He played the old game of sending a double to Chicago, and he was in Belgium before we knew the truth. There, from what we gather, he handed over the stuff to the old man and his sister, and took up his soldiering job. The worst of it is he's covered up his traces so well that we haven't a chance unless we can catch him, or one of the three, with the goods. Meanwhile, there he is, less than a quarter of a mile away, with half a million of loot under his nose; there's a reward of twenty-five thousand dollars for his apprehension; and here we three men sit, needing the money, and pretty well powerless."

"I wouldn't go so far as that," Harvey Grimm said quietly. "I don't fancy you've come to the end of your tether yet, Brodie."

The detective knocked the ash from his cigar and rose to his feet.

"Well," he admitted. "I ain't giving up, sure. All the same, this little failure has made things difficult for me. If I put my head in at headquarters and whisper 'Jeremiah Sands,' they're down my throat. I just looked in to see how you boys were," he added. "They'll have tumbled to you both now, so I'm afraid the game's off so far as you are concerned. So long! See you round at the Milan about cocktail time, Harvey, eh?"

Mr. Brodie took his leave, with more expressions of cordiality. Aaron Rodd closed the door carefully after him and came back into the room.

For several moments neither of the two men spoke. Harvey Grimm carefully selected a cigarette and lit it. Then he walked to the door, opened it and peered down the stairs.

"Too damned amiable!" he muttered, as he returned to his place. "Did you see the way he peered around? You have brightened things up a bit Aaron."

"I haven't done more than was absolutely necessary," the young lawyer protested. "The place was simply filthy."

Harvey Grimm suddenly burst into a hearty laugh and slapped his knee.

"That's all right, old fellow," he declared. "It don't matter a snap of the fingers. That chap Brodie does get me, though. A baby could see through him. He's got just sense enough to believe that we pinched the diamond— that's why he's been round here. It just don't matter a damn, Aaron, what he suspects. That diamond doesn't exist any longer. Neither our friends whom we—er—relieved of its incriminating possession, nor Paul Brodie, will ever see that stone again. Let's lunch."

Aaron Rodd reached for his hat and followed his friend out into the street At the end of the little dingy thoroughfare, as they made their way up towards the Strand, Harvey Grimm paused abruptly in front of what seemed to be a small book-shop. There were only one or two volumes in the window, of what seemed to be editions de luxe of some unknown work. There was a single modern engraving and a water-colour of Futurist propensities for background. Harvey Grimm eyed these treasures appreciatively.

"This place pleases me," he announced. "It has an air of its own. We will spend a few minutes here."

The two men entered and looked about them, a little bewildered by their surroundings. They seemed to have stepped into a small and feminine sitting-room, the walls of which were hung with water-colours of unusual subjects and colouring. There was a little pile of paper-covered volumes upon the table. A young lady of sombre and uncertain appearance came forward, and Harvey Grimm promptly removed his hat.

"We have perhaps made a mistake?" he observed tentatively. "From the exterior appearance of your establishment, I gathered that we might possibly be able to procure here something unusual in the way of literature. In a small way I am a collector of old books."

"We are entirely modern here," the young woman replied. "I can show you hand-made pottery, or the water-colours of a young Futurist artist, or I can offer you the poetical works of one or two of our most modern poets. Secondhand books or *objets d'art* we do not deal in. We consider," she concluded, "that modernity, absolute modernity, is the proper cult."

Harvey Grimm fanned himself for a moment with his hat His companion was gazing, with his mouth a little open, at a picture upon the wall which appeared to him to represent the bursting of a ripe tomato upon a crazy landscape.

"An impression of war," the young woman remarked, following his gaze. "A wonderful piece of work by a young Futurist painter."

Harvey Grimm studied it for a moment through his eyeglass, and coughed. He turned back to the table and picked up a paper-covered volume.

"Poetry," he murmured, "is one of my great solaces."

"Have you met with the work of Stephen Cresswell?" the young woman inquired, almost solemnly.

Harvey Grimm repeated the name several times.

"For the moment—" he confessed.

"Eightpence," the girl interrupted, depositing one of the paper-covered volumes in his hand. "Perhaps your friend would like one, too. I can promise you that when you have read Cresswell's *Spring Lyrics*, you will find all Victorian poetry anaemic."

Harvey Grimm handed a copy to his companion, laid down two shillings and pocketed the eightpence change a little diffidently.

"You would perhaps like to look around," the young lady suggested.

She vanished into an inner room. Almost at that moment the door leading into the street was violently opened, and a young man of somewhat surprising appearance abruptly entered. He was over six feet in height, he wore a flannel shirt and collar much the worse for wear, a brown tweed coat from which every button was missing, and through an old pair of patent boots came an unashamed and very evident toe. The two visitors stared at him in amazement. The young man's eyes, from the moment of his entrance, were fixed upon the paper volume which Harvey Grimm was carrying.

"Sir," he inquired, "am I to conclude that you have purchased a copy—the copy of poems you hold in your hand?"

"I have just done so," Harvey Grimm admitted; "also my friend."

The young man pushed past him towards the inner room.

"Bertha," he exclaimed loudly, "eightpence, please! You have sold two copies of my poems. The eightpence!"

There was a momentary silence and then the clinking of coins. The young man reappeared and made for the door with an air of determination in his face. Harvey Grimm tapped him on the shoulder.

"Sir," he said, "forgive me if I take a liberty, but am I right in presuming that you are the author of this volume?"

"I am," was the prompt reply, "and I am going to have a drink."

"One moment, if you please," his questioner begged. "This, you must remember, is an impertinent age. Modernity demands it. Are you not also hungry?"

"Ravenous," Mr. Stephen Cresswell confessed; "but what can one do with eightpence?"

"You will join my friend and myself," Harvey Grimm declared firmly. "We are going to take a chop."

The young man's tongue seemed to wander around the outside of his lips.

"A chop," he repeated absently.

"At a neighbouring grill-room," Harvey Grimm went on. "Come, I have bought two copies of your poems. I have a claim upon your consideration."

"Do I understand," the young man asked, "that you will pay for the chop?"

"That will be my privilege," was the prompt assertion.

"You are doubtless mad," the poet observed, "but you are probably opulent. Let us hurry."

They left the place and crossed the street, the young man in the middle. Aaron Rodd was speechless. His eyes seemed fascinated by the deficiencies of their new friend's toilet, a fact of which he himself seemed sublimely unconscious. Harvey Grimm, however, proceeded to make a delicate allusion to the matter.

"Some little accident, I gather," he remarked, "has happened—forgive my noticing it—to your right shoe."

The poet glanced carelessly downwards.

"It occurred this morning," he sighed. "To tell you the truth, I had scarcely noticed it. There was a green streak in the sunrise. I hastened—"

Harvey Grimm paused in front of a boot-shop.

"This place," he said firmly, "will do as well as another."

"Why not?" the young man agreed, entering promptly, seating himself upon the nearest vacant chair and holding out his foot. "Something light," he begged. "You will observe that my foot is long and narrow."

The shopman withdrew the tattered remnants of shoes and stared in amazement at his prospective customer's bare feet. The latter held out his hand for a cigarette and tapped it against the side of Harvey Grimm's case.

"It appears to me," he continued, gazing at his mud-stained feet, "that I came out without socks. The sunrise again. However, it is a deficiency which I perceive that you are in a position to remedy."

He selected without embarrassment a pair of socks and shoes, and was perfectly willing to don a tie which they purchased from a small haberdasher's shop at the end of the street. That affair disposed of, however, he became quite firm.

"The affair of the chop," he insisted.

"We are there," Harvey Grimm interrupted, leading him to an hotel grill-room.

The young man paused before the large open grid and carefully indicated the chop which he considered suitable for his consumption. He then seated himself opposite his two friends and expressed himself in favour of a mixed vermouth.

"A very pleasing encounter, this," he declared, drawing the eightpence from his pocket and looking at it thoughtfully. "May I ask, sir, whether you are acquainted with my poems?"

"Not yet," Harvey Grimm confessed.

"Your purchase, then, was accidental?"

"Entirely," his patron explained. "My friend and I are adventurers. We seek the unusual. The appearance of the shop where we met you attracted us. The young lady to whom we addressed some inquiries tendered us a copy of your verses."

The young man sighed.

"It is a scandalous thing," he said, "to be published in paper covers at eightpence—fourpence to the author. So you are adventurers. You mean by that thieves?"

"Sir," Aaron Rodd interrupted, "I am a solicitor."

"My ignorance," the young man declared, "is amazing, but that, I presume, is a legalised form of robbery? I am one of the few persons in the world who give value for the money I earn. I produce, create. If only ten thousand people in the city were to pay eightpence for a copy of my works. I should be affluent, as you two are. I should lunch here every day and drink Burgundy."

"Then in a very short time," Harvey Grimm reminded him, "you would cease to write poetry."

His protégé shook his head.

"A well-nurtured body is an incentive to poetic thought," he insisted. "There is a richness of imagery which comes with after-dinner composing; a sort of mental starvation, an anaemic scantiness of similes, which follows the fruit luncheon and cold water of necessity. Adventurers, gentlemen, are you? That is to say you are people with wits. Tell me, then—bring me an idea from the practical world—how shall I make ten thousand people buy a copy of my poems?"

"Come, that's an interesting problem," Harvey Grimm declared. "Of course, if one were to answer you in a single word, that one word would be Advertisement."

"If I could write my name across the heavens, or flash it from a million lights through the clouds," the young man remarked, "I would do so, but these things call for either miraculous powers or money. I have neither."

"Your case," Harvey Grimm promised, "shall have our attention, my friend's and mine. In the meantime, the moment seems opportune, pending the arrival of our chops, for a glance at your work. Permit me."

The poetaster crossed his legs, leaned back in his chair, thrust an eyeglass into his eye and turned over the pages of the paper volume which he had been carrying. Aaron Rodd followed his example. The poet, entirely unembarrassed, eyed hungrily each covered dish which passed. At the arrival of their meal. Harvey Grimm solemnly pocketed his book and replaced his eyeglass. Aaron Rodd went on reading for a moment. Then he glanced surreptitiously at their guest and laid his volume face downwards upon the table.

"Your poems, I perceive," Harvey Grimm observed, as he helped himself to a potato, "are not written for the man in the street."

"They are written," the poet declared, falling hungrily upon his chop, "for any one who will pay eightpence for them."

Conversation faded away. It was not until the service of coffee and cigars that anything more than disjointed words were spoken. The young man's face was still colourless but his eyes were less hard. He took out his pencil and toyed for a moment with the menu.

"Some little trifle," he suggested, "commemorative of the occasion?"

"I would rather," Harvey Grimm confessed, "think out some scheme for advertising your work. There's a little thing here about a lame busman—"

"Any scheme you suggest," the young man assented dreamily. "I frankly admit that the dispersal of my productions is a matter in which I have failed. The appreciative few may have purchased, but the man of the day passes on, ignorant of the great need he really has of poetry. Ten thousand copies of my poems, sold in London, would produce at once a more gracious spirit. You would observe a difference in the deportment, the speech, the greater altruism of the multitude. How shall I force my works into their hands and their eightpence into my pocket?"

"Fourpence only," Aaron Rodd reminded him. "The publishers get half."

"In the event of a large circulation," the poet pointed out, with a wave of the hand, "better terms might be arrived at. You, as a legal man, can appreciate that possibility."

"There is only one idea which occurs to me," Harvey Grimm declared, after a brief pause. "Come, and we will make an experiment."

They marched out into the streets and walked solemnly along towards Leicester Square. Suddenly Harvey Grimm stopped short and accosted a small grey-haired man who was carrying a bag and walking quickly.

"I beg your pardon, sir," the former began.

"What is it?" the little man demanded.

Harvey Grimm took him gently by the lapel of his coat. The little man seemed too surprised to resist.

"I want the privilege of a few minutes' conversation with you," Harvey Grimm continued. "You are one of the uneducated ten thousand who, on behalf of my friend here. Stephen Cresswell, the great poet, I am anxious to reach. Have you read Cresswell's poems?"

"I am in a hurry," the little man insisted, gazing at his interlocutor in a bewildered manner, and struggling to escape.

"The whole world is in a hurry," Harvey Grimm observed, drawing the paper volume from his pocket with the other hand. "This volume of poems will cost you eightpence. It will bring relief to its impoverished author, you yourself will become an enlightened—"

"I wish you'd let me go," the little man protested angrily. "I don't know you, and I don't want to stand about the streets, talking to a stranger, Let me go or I'll call a policeman."

"A policeman can afford you no assistance," Harvey Grimm assured him. "I shall remain polite but insistent. You will buy this volume of poems for eightpence, or—"

"Or what?" his victim demanded. Harvey Grimm leaned down and whispered in his car. The little man's hand shot into his pocket. He produced sixpence and two coppers, snatched at the book and hurried off. The victor in this little *rencontre* turned to his companions with an air of triumph and handed the eightpence to the poet, who immediately pocketed it.

"The whole problem is solved," he declared.

"You are a great man, sir," the poet exclaimed, grasping him by the hand; "but what was it you whispered in his ear?"

"I simply told him," Harvey Grimm said blandly, "that I should biff him one. The cost of a new hat is ten and sixpence; the price of your poems is eightpence."

"You are a great man, sir," the poet repeated heartily. "Watch the newspapers."

* * * *

With a bunch of early violets in his buttonhole, neatly and correctly dressed from the crown of his hat to his patent boots. Mr. Harvey Grimm, one morning about a fortnight later, turned down the narrow street which led to his friend Aaron Rodd's office. He took a few steps and paused in surprise. A little crowd encumbered the pavement in front of him. There were at least half a dozen taxicabs waiting by the side of the pavement. A printer's van was busy unloading. A constant procession, consisting chiefly of elderly and middle-aged men, were entering and leaving the little book-shop. Waiting his turn, Harvey Grimm stepped in. The whole of the central table was taken up by great piles of a little paper-covered volume, recognisable at once as the Poetical Works of Stephen Cresswell, and as fast as the flow of customers could be served, they departed with one or more copies in their pockets. The young lady, whose hair was more untidy than ever, and who wore a stupefied air, doled them out in doll-like and mechanical fashion. She had lost her air of superiority. She pointed no longer to the sketches upon the walls or the pottery beyond. She behaved like a dazed automaton. Now and then Harvey Grimm could hear her reply to inquiries.

"There will be a cloth edition of Mr. Cresswell's works out in a few days," she said. "The printers have promised them by the end of the week."

In the background were two very obvious newspaper men, waiting, so far unsuccessfully, to get in a word with her. Mr. Harvey Grimm elbowed his way by some means or other into the line, paid his eightpence and retired into the recesses of the little suite of rooms beyond for a moment's breathing-space. A rush of at least a dozen old gentlemen had made exit temporarily impossible. As he stood and watched the scene, he was conscious of a fashionably dressed young man lounging in an easy-chair a few yards away. The young man suddenly arose.

"My benefactor!" he cried.

Harvey Grimm gripped his copy of poems tightly and held it up.

"Pax!" he exclaimed. "I have one."

The poet smiled wearily. He drew his erstwhile patron a little farther back into the most retired portion of the premises.

"Listen," he said; "this has been the most stupendous, the most colossal joke of the day. On the first night I sandbagged a wholesale provision merchant, who admitted that he had never read my poems, and he wrote to the *Times* the next morning. I made myself objectionable to seven others the following night. They, too, made various complaints. After that I retired—their description of my identity was becoming embarrassing."

Mr. Harvey Grimm was a little puzzled.

"But the thing has been going on right up till last night," he declared. "The papers for days have been a source of joy to me."

"After the first few nights," the young man explained, "I was compelled to engage substitutes, have acquaintances whose life has been spent—shall we say—on the fringe of things? With their aid I made the acquaintance of various professional gentlemen from the East-End, who for a suitable remuneration took up this business with avidity. They were of all sizes, and they operated in all localities, choosing their victims, so far as possible, with discretion. There was but one question—'Have you read the poems of Stephen Cresswell?'—generally a bewildered negative, and then biff! The people began frantically to inquire who was Stephen Cresswell, where were his poems to be obtained? People who had the slightest pretensions to literary knowledge were assailed with questions. *Punch*—"

"I saw *Punch*," Mr. Harvey Grimm interrupted. "Very clever!"

"Then the stream began," the young man continued. "I can assure you that from opening time till dark, this place is mobbed. You see, on the third night a confederate was saved from an imaginary assault by promptly producing a copy of my poems. He wrote to the paper in mock indignation, but describing his escape. Then the rush began. Eleven thousand copies have been sold, some at a premium. Eleven thousand fourpences have found their way into my pocket. A morocco-bound and vellum-covered edition are waiting in the Press for one thing."

"And that?"

"The name of my benefactor. I wish to dedicate the third, fourth, and fifth editions of my poems to you," the young man declared grandiloquently.

Mr. Harvey Grimm pondered.

"It is an immense compliment," he acknowledged. "We will talk of it."

"In the meantime," the poet went on, "listen. The curse of these days is jealousy and imitation. A young man of worthy upbringing, but wholly ignorant of art, who perpetrated the daubs which you see upon the walls here, was struck with my success. Only last Thursday an elderly gentleman, such a one as might have been selected by my own employees, was stopped in Hampstead and asked whether he had seen the sketches of Sidney Wentworth, displayed in Manchester Street, Adelphi. The fool admitted that he had never heard of them, and down he went. I ask you, sir, was there ever a more flagrant case of spoiling a man's market? From the moment this absurd affair was reported, public feeling has begun to change. Curiously enough, there has been very small resentment, even on the part of those who have suffered slight pains in the cause of art, as to my methods, Now, however, that the idea has commenced to spread that such means are becoming a regular curriculum of the advertiser, I have noticed distinct expressions of indignation. In plain words. I can see the end coming."

"Nothing lasts," Mr. Harvey Grimm pointed out, "and you must admit you've had a run for your money."

"I've had more than that, sir," the poet admitted. "I am established. Many of the leading periodicals of the day have invited me to contribute to their pages. The Society of Authors has made me a tempting proposition to join their ranks. You may look upon me, sir, as a man whose future is now assured."

"I am delighted to hear it," Mr. Harvey Grimm declared heartily. "I fear I must now be getting on."

The young man took down his hat, possessed himself of a pair of expensive doeskin gloves and a silver-topped cane.

"I will let you out by the back way," he suggested. "It is my desire to accompany you."

"I am going to call upon a friend in the neighbourhood," Harvey Grimm remarked.

"The friend with whom I met you first?"

"The same."

"I shall accompany you," the young man announced, cautiously opening a side door and peering up and down a stone-flagged passage. "The way is clear, sir. Come with me."

They sallied out and found themselves in the street. The young man gripped the arm of his companion.

"For the moment," he confessed. "I am weary of poetry. I seek life. You are an adventurer, you have told me. I shall link my fortune with yours. You have a brain, sir, enterprise, and I should imagine that you are untrammelled by the modern conscience. I am in the same position. Poetry is affording me, for some time, at least, the means of sustenance. Let us go together a little farther afield."

The older man looked his companion up and down. He was a strong, well-built young fellow, and the hollows of his cheeks had already filled out. Notwithstanding his mannerisms, he was without doubt a young man of resolution.

"We will see," Harvey Grimm suggested, "what Aaron Rodd has to say about it."

"I like your friend's name," the young man declared solemnly. "I am sure that he will accept me as a comrade."

They trod the few remaining yards of pavement, ascended the stone stairs, and, after a preliminary knock at the door, Harvey Grimm, exercising the privilege of familiarity, turned the handle and stepped inside, followed by his companion. For a single moment neither of them spoke. Harvey Grimm's first conscious action was to close the door behind him. Then they stood inside the apartment, transfixed. Around them was a scene of the wildest disorder. The linoleum had been torn up and thrown into a corner, planks had been torn bodily from the floor, the cupboards stood open and their contents were thrown right and left. The little row of tin boxes stood on their sides, and masses of dusty parchment littered the whole place. Seated in chair before the desk was Aaron Rodd, with a gag in his mouth, his arms bound behind him, his legs tied together. His face was livid, his eyes half closed. He showed no signs of life at their coming. The poet produced a knife.

"We must set him free," he said.

His companion, subconsciously amazed at the young man's initiative, followed him to the desk. Methodically the latter, having removed the gag from Aaron Rodd's mouth, cut the bonds which held him, one by one. Harvey Grimm produced a small brandy flask and held it to his lips. The poet threw open a window and swung the chair round. Aaron Rodd groaned.

"He is coming to," Cresswell remarked hopefully.

He caught up a sheaf of newspapers and fanned the swooning man vigorously. Then he suddenly paused. Harvey Grimm followed the direction of his gaze. A sheet of violet-coloured notepaper was pinned upon the desk. The poet sniffed.

"What a delicious odour!" he murmured. "And how familiar!"

They both approached a little nearer. The sheet of notepaper, fluttering a little in the breeze which streamed through the window, gave out the subtlest and most delicate perfume—a perfume which seemed like a waft from a field of violets, carried on a west wind. There were only a few words, writdten in a delicate feminine handwriting:

> *"Should there not be honour,*
> *even amongst thieves?"*

The young man struck a theatrical attitude.

"Fate has sent me to join you," he declared, waving his hand towards the sheet of violet-coloured paper. "I recognise the handwriting. I know well the perfume. I can tell you who wrote that note."

CHAPTER III

AN ALLIANCE OF THIEVES

Aaron Rodd was walking along the, to him, unfamiliar thoroughfare of Bond Street when he was suddenly confronted with a vision. A large limousine motorcar was drawn up just in front of him. An elderly lady with white hair, leaning upon the arm of a powdered footman, crossed the pavement, followed by a girl who was smothered in sables, carried a small dog under her arm, and wore a great bunch of violets partially concealed by her furs. Aaron Rodd's abrupt pause was not one of politeness alone. With an eagerness which took no account of manners or discretion, he gazed at the girl, open-eyed, open-mouthed, blankly, unashamed. If anything were left to complete his bewilderment, it was the little smile upon her lips as she met his eyes.

"Good afternoon, Mr. Aaron Rodd!" she murmured, as she passed.

She disappeared through the swing doors of the shop. Aaron stared after her as though expecting a backward glance, stared at the very handsome motorcar, at what appeared to be a coronet upon the panel, at the imperturbable expression of the powdered footman, standing with a rug over his arm, looking into vacancy. Then he limped on a few feet and devoted himself to an absorbed contemplation of some Japanese trifles in a curio shop.

He lost count of time in his firm determination to await her return. As a matter of fact, it was only a very few minutes before he was conscious of her reappearance. She hesitated for a moment on the threshold of the shop, shook her head at the footman who was already opening the door of the car, and approached Aaron Rodd. He turned abruptly from the window and greeted her with grave politeness. She glanced at his left arm, still in a sling; at the heavy walking-stick by which he supported himself.

"Good-afternoon. Mr. Rodd," she said. "You have met, perhaps, with a little accident? It is so?"

"Your friends were a little rough," he replied.

"I shall be annoyed with them," she promised. "You received my message?"

"Certainly," he replied. "On the whole I agree with you."

She shrugged her shoulders.

"And what are you doing in Bond Street?" she asked him.

"I am on my way to meet my friend Harvey Grimm."

She nodded.

"That is your clever confederate, who stole our diamond," she remarked suavely.

"A very fortunate circumstance for you," he ventured to remind her. "If that stone—the real one, I mean—had been discovered in your possession at the police station, I fancy that your position in this country would have become a little difficult."

"Oh, la, la!" she laughed. "You should have seen the face of Mr. Brodie, though, when they examined the imitation stone! I do not think that the English police are pleased with him. They were very kind to my grandfather and me."

"Nevertheless," he advised, "if I were your brother, I think that I would keep away from London just now."

"And why?"

Aaron Rodd glanced up and down the pavement to be sure that there were no listeners.

"That fellow Brodie is not such a fool as he seems," he declared. "He has made one mistake. I do not think that he is likely to make another."

She laughed.

"If it is to be a duel of wits," she murmured, "between Leopold and Mr. Brodie, do you know, I believe that Leopold will win."

"There is such a thing as over-confidence," he reminded her.

"I have so many ways," she told him, with twinkling eyes, "of diverting these people from the scent. Do you recognise the old lady upon whom I am in attendance today, the old lady who went with me into that shop?"

"I have not that pleasure," he replied grimly. "Is she one of the gang?"

"She is a royal princess—the Princess Augusta. If you do not believe me, look in this week's *Tatler*, and you will see her picture—perhaps mine. You are a very funny man, Mr. Aaron Rodd, and you have treated us very badly indeed, but I like you—yes, I like you quite well. How much money did you get for that stone you stole from us?"

The colour mounted mercilessly to his temples. He seemed suddenly bereft of words.

"Do not be foolish," she continued quickly. "Really, as you know, I am an adventuress myself, and I rather admire you both. I think that we ought to make friends. You could be of great service to us. There is no need for us to quarrel because you have had the best of this first little exchange. What do you say to that, my friend?"

Aaron Rodd found himself and became once more a man. He looked her squarely in the eyes.

"I would rather be friends with you," he said, "than any one in the world."

For a moment the triumph was his. It was she who was almost embarrassed by his directness. Then intervention came.

"Ah!" she exclaimed, "the Princess! *Au revoir!*"

She stepped lightly away from him, with a little nod of farewell. The footman stood bareheaded as he opened the door of the car. One of the principals of the establishment which the grey-haired lady had just quitted stood bowing upon the pavement. In the face of all this, the girl turned deliberately around and waved her hand as the car drove off. Aaron Rodd limped down Bond Street, called for a taxi and drove to the Milan Court....

His two auditors listened to Aaron Rodd's story with varying expressions—the poet with pleased and affable sympathy; Harvey Grimm, on the other hand, with obvious irritation. They were seated in a corner of the smoke-room, and the latter at once dispatched a waiter for a copy of the *Tatler*. When it arrived, they all three pored over one of the leading illustrations. There was no doubt whatever in the minds of any of the three men as to the identity of the girl who was depicted as being amongst the ladies-in-waiting of a royal personage.

"That," the poet declared, "is a young lady whose name is Henriette de Floge. She has an underhand service at Badminton and she wants to learn to be a futurist. She attended a class last year, organised by an artist friend of mine in Chelsea. Ye gods!"

"That, without a single doubt," Aaron Rodd asserted, laying his forefinger upon the illustration, "is the young lady who was in attendance this afternoon upon the Princess Augusta."

"And it is equally and absolutely and conclusively certain," Harvey Grimm pronounced, "that she came to Manchester Street, Adelphi, as the confederate of Jeremiah Sands."

"Who," the poet asked eagerly, "is Jeremiah Sands? I like the name."

"Jeremiah Sands," Harvey Grimm told him, "is the head and the brains of the smallest but most formidable band of criminals who have ever succeeded in eluding justice for nearly ten years. There is a reward of twenty-five thousand dollars for his arrest in America, and he is wanted in most of the capitals of Europe. He has a dozen aliases and a score of personalities. This much about him is certain. He is either of Belgian or French birth, he is a young man, and he has spent the greater part of the last seven years in America. The universal excuse given by the police of every country for their failure to apprehend him is that, for at any rate the last five years, he has simply accumulated his booty and has made no effort to dispose of it. As you know, most of the thieves of the world are traced backwards through the receiver of stolen goods. His last exploit in New York was the theft of the Van Hutten jewels. It was, without a doubt, one of those diamonds which was—mislaid in Aaron Rodd's office, and it was one of Jeremiah Sands' agents who paid our friend here that last domiciliary visit in search of it."

"What, by the by, became of that diamond?" the poet inquired.

"We are living upon it," Mr. Harvey Grimm confessed.

The poet sighed enviously. "It is a beautiful existence," he declared. "When are we going to embark upon another adventure of the sort?"

"The aftermath of the last one is still enveloping us," Mr. Harvey Grimm reminded him. "There is Scotland Yard, who have seen the imitation stone and who suspect us of changing it. Then there is Mr. Jeremiah Sands, who knows that we did, and who is only just beginning to realise that we have been clever enough to dispose of it. Finally, there is Mr. Brodie, the amateur detective, who has the same idea and who is furious with us for letting him down with the authorities. Between the three, you see, our position is a little difficult. Personally, I am much interested in our friend Aaron's account of his conversation with the young lady. Her suggestion of some measure of alliance appeals to me."

"And me," the poet agreed. "Let us approach them at once. I should like to come into contact with this Jeremiah Sands."

There was a brief interval whilst a waiter deposited before them a tray of cocktails, subtly ordered by the poet by means of sundry evolutions with his forefinger. Afterwards, Mr. Harvey Grimm sat for a few moments in silence, smoothing out his immaculate doeskin gloves.

"Listen," he said presently, after a cautious glance around the room. "I will tell you my impressions. Jeremiah Sands has never been caught, for two reasons—first, because he has stored up all his booty and has never been in the hands of the receivers; secondly, because he has hiding-places in every capital of Europe, all of them safer than London or New York. At the present moment he is like a rabbit which has been ferreted out of its hole. Europe is suddenly closed to him. He has been driven to London. He is ill-at-ease here. He has lost many of his agents. To maintain his Belgian nationality he has been forced into the army. The perfect machinery of his wonderful system must be seriously dislocated. The time, too, has probably arrived when he finds it necessary to dispose of some of his plunder. Let us offer him a tentative amity."

Aaron Rodd frowned.

"Do you think that he would trust us after that last little affair? I don't mind being the thief or the thief-catcher," he added bluntly, "but I rather hate being the third party."

"The only party we have to consider is ourselves," Harvey Grimm replied deliberately. "To tell you the truth, I fear that we have lost the confidence of Paul Brodie. I am not sure whether it would be worth our while to try and regain it. The sharing of rewards is a poor game. I would rather hear what Jeremiah Sands has to say."

He took up his pencil and scrawled a few lines across a half-sheet of notepaper. They both looked over his shoulder:

If the young lady with violets would like to resume her conversation with a certain person in Bond Street this morning, please reply in Friday's "Telegraph."

"I propose," Mr. Harvey Grimm explained, "to insert this in tomorrow morning's *Telegraph*, to send a copy here to Mr. Brinnen and await results."

"Brilliant!" the poet exclaimed. "It gives the proper flavour to the whole thing. But why not write a note and send it up by the waiter?"

Mr. Harvey Grimm smiled.

"My young friend," he said, "you are an adventurer of the bulldog type. Let me tell you this. I happen to know it to be a fact. From the moment when Mr. Paul Brodie communicated his suspicions, as to our friends, to Scotland Yard, their every movement, and without doubt their correspondence, has been closely watched. I will guarantee to you that not a letter is delivered to either Captain Leopold Brinnen, to Mr. Brinnen, or to the young lady, which docs not run a very considerable risk of being opened."

The poet listened with a pleased smile.

"I like the flavour of this sort of thing," he acknowledged. "Let us insert the advertisement, by all means. If the young lady suggests a meeting, I shall recommend myself as the most suitable person to keep the appointment."

* * * *

Soon after midday, two mornings later, Mr. Stephen Cresswell entered the smoking-room at the Milan. He was carrying a *Daily Telegraph* under his arm, he wore a bunch of violets in his buttonhole, and he was dressed with great care. He approached the table where Harvey Grimm and Aaron Rodd were awaiting him.

"You, too, have seen the answer to our advertisement?" he exclaimed. "Capital!"

"We were just now discussing it," Harvey Grimm assented.

The poet sat down, made signs to the waiter, hitched up his trousers and made himself thoroughly comfortable.

"I have decided," he announced, "that I am the proper person to entertain the young lady."

Harvey Grimm nodded thoughtfully.

"Tell us through what channel of thought, my young friend, you have arrived at that conclusion?" he begged.

The poet straightened his tie. There was no doubt that he was a remarkably good-looking young man.

"I am a modest person," he said, "but it is useless to deny that nature has been kind to me. Then, too, there is a peculiar and romantic importance attached to the successful poet whose reputation has been enhanced in so singular a fashion. The young lady will be interested in me from the start. She will be proud to remember that we are old acquaintances, and she will treat me with greater confidence than any ordinary person."

Harvey Grimm lit a cigarette deliberately. Aaron Rodd's heavy eyebrows seemed to have contracted a little.

"Why are you so sure that it will be the young lady who will keep the appointment?" the former inquired.

Stephen Cresswell placed his forefinger upon the advertisement in the paper which he had been carrying:

Milan Café, luncheon, 1.15 Wednesday. Will discuss. Bond Street.

"That tells us nothing," Harvey Grimm pointed out. "So far as the probabilities are concerned, I should say that it is extremely unlikely that either the young lady or any of those associated with her will keep the appointment. Any negotiations we may have will probably be conducted through a third party."

The poet's face fell. He ordered another cocktail brusquely.

"How shall we know whom to look out for, then?" he demanded.

"The onus of recognition will rest with the others," Harvey Grimm replied. "I have engaged a table just inside the door. We shall take our places there before one-fifteen and await the arrival of whoever may come."

"In case it should be the young lady," the poet persisted, "you would find that my previous acquaintance with her would be of immense service to us. She would place confidence in me."

"You shall be of the party," Harvey Grimm promised. "I have ordered the table for five, so as to be on the safe side. I do not understand our friend's selecting so public a place for a meeting, but, on the other hand, there is a flavour of genius in such apparent recklessness. If you are ready, I think it is time that we made a start."

They strolled down to the cafe and took their places at a table just inside the door. At precisely a quarter past one a little tremor of excitement suddenly unloosed their tongues.

"My God!" Harvey Grimm muttered.

"They must be mad!" Aaron Rodd whispered, in a hoarse undertone.

"It is Henriette de Floge," Stephen Cresswell murmured complacently. "You will perceive soon the advantage of my presence."

The girl approached their table smilingly. She was followed by the young officer in Belgian uniform. The three men rose to their feet. She smiled pleasantly at Aaron Rodd.

"You have not yet met my brother, have you?" she asked. "Let me present Captain Leopold Brinnen—Mr. Aaron Rodd, Mr. Harvey Grimm, and—"

She paused, with her eyes fixed questioningly upon the poet. The young officer had brought his heels together and bowed ceremoniously to the two men.

"I am not, I hope, forgotten," the poet observed. "My name is Stephen Cresswell. I have had the pleasure of playing Badminton with you in Walter Donne's studio."

She looked across at him with slightly upraised eyebrows, the faint tracings of a somewhat insolent smile at the corners of her lips.

"Badminton? Is that an English game? I perceive that I have a double. I have not played it."

"You are Mademoiselle de Floge?" the poet persisted.

She shook her head gently.

"On the contrary," she replied, "I am Henriette Brinnen. Leopold, this is Mr. Stephen Cresswell."

They all took their places, the poet a little heavily. His stupefaction, even though it proceeded from a different cause, was only a little less profound than that of the other two. Mr. Harvey Grimm took up the menu once more and gave a few murmured orders to the *maître d'hôtel*. Aaron Rodd, who was on her right-hand side, leaned towards the girl. His face was almost haggard with anxiety.

"Forgive me," he whispered, "but is this wise? Have you counted the cost of it?"

"I do not understand," she answered, a little vaguely.

"You know that we are all watched," he reminded her. "We thought it best, even, not to communicate with you direct."

"You three are such droll men," she laughed. "There is your nice-looking friend, Mr. Stephen Cresswell, who sits there and will not take his eyes off me. He does not believe that he has never met me before. And Mr. Harvey Grimm—well, he does not seem a nervous person, does he, and just now he is almost pale. And you, too—you speak with bated breath of risks and being watched. How, then, do you carry through your great coups, my friend? Have you not learnt the first axiom of the adventurer—there is nothing which dispels suspicion so readily as candour?"

Aaron Rodd shrugged his shoulders and busied himself with the task of attending to his companion's wants. Conversation around the little table became platitudinal. The three men, although they behaved in all respects reasonably, were unable to keep their thoughts and attention from wandering continually towards their slim, grave-looking young guest in his somewhat tattered uniform, who seemed chiefly engrossed with his luncheon. It was hard to believe that he sat there in one of the best-known restaurants in the world, with a great price upon his head. In some respects he was like his sister, Aaron Rodd decided, although there was a curious virility of expression which flashed sometimes into his features, and a more calculating light in his hard, clear eyes. His mouth was unusually long, straight and thin, his cheek-bones a little high. One could believe that, notwithstanding his inconsiderable stature, his frame was like steel. He spoke English very deliberately, with now and then the slightest American accent, but on the few occasions when he addressed his sister it seemed to be a relief for him to relapse into French. It was not until the coffee was served that he leaned a little towards Harvey Grimm and dispelled by a few words the atmosphere of unreality which had somehow or other hovered over the little luncheon-party.

"Sir," he proposed, "let us approach the object of this meeting."

"With pleasure," Harvey Grimm assented.

"For some reason or other," the young man continued, "my sister, although, as we know to our cost, her acquaintance with you so far has not been altogether profitable, has confidence in you. Let us speak frankly. You gentlemen, I believe, are what is generally known as *chevaliers d'industrie?*"

There was a sudden flush of colour in Aaron Rodd's cheeks. The poet, who was a little sullen, distinctly scowled. Only Harvey Grimm bowed placidly, seemingly unconscious of the faint note of contempt in the other's tone.

"In the ordinary sense of the word, that is true," he admitted.

"Consider, then, our position," the young man continued. "My grandfather and sister, whom I meet again after an absence of some years, owing to the haste with which they were compelled to leave Belgium, are almost penniless. My own—savings consist of perhaps half a million pounds' worth of diamonds. These jewels," he went on, knocking the ash from his cigarette, "have all been stolen. They can only be disposed of in an irregular fashion. That is to say, the stones must be re-cut. In normal times, this problem would present no difficulties to me. Today, when London is the only capital of Europe open to us, I must admit that I find myself in a difficult position. The few artificers in this country are, I understand, well known and watched. I am bound, therefore, to employ an agent. Under the peculiar circumstances to which I have alluded, I cannot seek for an honest man. I am prepared to make it worth the while of men such as yourselves to deal honestly with me."

"My brother has your English gift of plain speech, you see," the girl whispered soothingly to Aaron Rodd.

The young officer lit a fresh cigarette and watched the smoke curl upward for a moment.

"Surely it is best?" he said softly. "These gentlemen are at the present moment living, and living, no doubt, exceedingly well, upon the proceeds of one of my diamonds. They should not, therefore, be sensitive."

"I may be allowed to remind you, sir," Harvey Grimm interrupted, "that, incidentally, the little artifice by means of which we secured it is responsible for your—unhindered presence here today."

"I take that fact into consideration," Leopold Brinnen assented, "in the toleration with which I view the circumstance. The point is, are you willing to deal with me?"

"I am perfectly willing to do so, sir," Harvey Grimm replied. "I am willing, too, and so, I am sure, are my friends, to take a certain amount of risk. I may add that I am probably the only man in England who can dispose of your jewels so that they cannot be traced. But before we proceed further, let me ask you a question. Are you aware, sir, of your position? There is an amateur detective here from New York, named Paul Brodie, who has no other object in life than to lay his hands upon a certain person. Scotland Yard, although just now they are a little fed up with Mr. Brodie, have very definite intentions with regard to the same person. You are living here openly. You are even flaunting your well-known Belgian uniform. There are eyes upon us as we sit at this table. There are eyes upon you and your sister and your grandfather, from the moment you rise in the morning till the moment you retire at night. Your rooms are at all times subject or liable to be searched. Any place you might visit is liable to be searched. Let me ask you, then, a plain question. More than any other quality I admire courage. Don't you think, however, that you are playing a little too near to the fire?"

The young officer stroked his thin black moustache. He had listened to Harvey Grimm's words attentively. He even indicated, in the slow movement of his head, some measure of approbation.

"To all that you have said, Mr. Harvey Grimm, I can make you only one reply," he said. "Every step which I have taken in life has been carefully thought out. The present position, although necessity has here intervened to some extent, has been subject to the same attentive consideration. I am safer than you think. Let that be enough. That I have friends is proved by the little visitation which was made upon Mr. Aaron Rodd the other day. I offer you no apologies, sir," he continued, bowing across the table. "It was part of the game. When we thrust the law outside our lives, as you have done and I, then we must take our knocks philosophically. For the future, however, even though we play the thieves' game, there is no reason why we should not play it honestly."

"A very admirable sentiment," the poet murmured.

"To put this matter upon a business basis, Mr. Grimm," Captain Brinnen continued, "supposing I supply you with a certain quantity of diamonds, will you guarantee to have them cut so as to render them unrecognisable, dispose of them, hand me two-thirds of the proceeds and retain a third yourself?"

"I have worked before upon those terms," Harvey Grimm replied. "I accept them. There is one little matter, though, to be cleared up."

Captain Brinnen smiled grimly.

"I fancy that I follow you," he observed. "You refer to the mysterious disappearance of a diamond from your friend's office?"

Harvey Grimm coughed.

"Bearing in mind, as I took the liberty of pointing out a few minutes ago, that its disappearance saved you from considerable inconvenience—" he began.

"The affair is finished," Brinnen interrupted. "Carry out faithfully the other transactions which we may arrange, and we will adopt—shall I say a resigned attitude?—with regard to that incident. When are you prepared to deal with the first parcel of stones?"

"At any moment," Harvey Grimm promised. "You will bring them to me?"

The girl, who had been listening eagerly to their conversation, leaned across the table.

"I think," she said, "that this time you had better come and fetch them, Mr. Grimm, or, better still—send Mr. Aaron Rodd."

"Or me," the poet suggested.

She shook her head.

"It is to be Mr. Aaron Rodd," she decided. "You will not be afraid?" she added, turning towards him with a little smile at the corners of her lips.

"Where am I to come to, and when?" he inquired.

She glanced at her brother, then back again towards her neighbour.

"I shall tell you presently," she whispered.

The little party broke up shortly afterwards. The hall outside, where they lingered to make their adieux, was unusually crowded. Harvey Grimm felt a touch upon his elbow.

"A pleasant luncheon, I trust?"

He frowned as he recognised Brodie, who was apparently waiting for a friend. It was exactly the meeting which he had desired to avoid. He greeted him, however, with his customary geniality.

"Lunching late, aren't you?" he observed.

Brodie seemed scarcely to hear him. His eyes were fixed upon the young Belgian, who, with his arm in a sling, was being helped carefully into his overcoat. Suddenly, however, he stretched out his arm, laid it upon Harvey Grimm's shoulder and drew him to within whispering distance.

"See here, Harvey," he muttered, "I don't know what game you're playing, but if any man tries to boost me, he's going to have a rough journey."

Harvey Grimm was shocked.

"My dear fellow!—" he began.

"Don't waste your breath," the other interrupted, as he turned away. "Remember, I've got my eye on you, as well as our friend there. It may be a waiting game, but you'll find me there at the finish, sure as my name's Paul Brodie."

He strode off towards the telephone booth. Harvey Grimm found his hand gripped by his guest.

"My sister and I thank you for a very excellent luncheon, Mr. Grimm," Captain Brinnen said politely. "I trust that you will soon give us an opportunity of repaying your hospitality."

"You will come to me," the girl whispered in Aaron Rodd's ear, "at number 13, Grosvenor Square, this afternoon at five o'clock."

* * * *

The poet was inclined to be peevish as the three men walked down the Strand.

"In this adventure," he declared, "I do not see where I come in. Aaron Rodd is to go and fetch the diamonds, and probably have tea with the beautiful young lady who has changed her name, and you," he went on, addressing Harvey Grimm, "thereupon vanish with the stones to your mysterious treasure-house and return with the gold. I am simply not in it. I might as well not exist."

"It is regrettable but true," Harvey Grimm assented. "Remember, however, that you are a self-invited newcomer to our little circle. A place shall be found for you presently. I can promise you that the cycle of our adventures will not be ended with the realisation of Jeremiah Sands' diamonds. This affair, unfortunately, presents no opportunity for your activities. I do not propose, even, to offer you more than a trifling share in the financial results."

"Financially," the poet announced airily, "I am independent. The taste for my poetry has spread like a forest fire. There will be a trifle of mine, by the by, in the *Pall Mall* tonight. Don't forget to look out for it."

Harvey Grimm for once was unsympathetic.

"Look here," he said, stopping suddenly, "I wish you'd forget your poetry for a few minutes. There is just one way you can make yourself useful. You saw a sleek, podgy, bulky, fat-faced-looking man, with hair brushed back, who spoke to me in the hall at the Milan?" The poet nodded.

"I remember," he murmured, "wishing that you would allow me to edit your acquaintances."

"That man," Harvey Grimm continued, "was Paul Brodie, an amateur detective. He has set himself the task of bringing about the arrest of Jeremiah Sands. He came to Europe with that idea. It was he who had the old gentleman and his daughter taken to the police station from my rooms. We have been working together, but he's out with us now, and he blames us for that fiasco. I should like to know why he is still hanging about the Milan Court."

"I will return there," the poet promised. "I will endeavour to engage him in conversation."

Harvey Grimm smiled pityingly.

"Oh, my ingenuous youth!" he murmured. "Your ideas of tackling a detective are bright and engaging, yet do your best. The very imbecility of your methods may lead to success. I should very much like to know where Paul Brodie is proposing to spend this afternoon."

Cresswell nodded in mysterious fashion and left them. Harvey Grimm passed his arm through his friend's as they turned into the little street which led down to Aaron Rodd's offices.

"Aaron," he said earnestly, "if your little expedition this afternoon should by any chance involve you in any manner of trouble, remember that there's one golden motto—silence. You make a cult of it in private life. If anything should happen to you—don't depart from it."

* * * *

At precisely the appointed hour, Aaron Rodd was shown by a footman in deep black livery into a small but charmingly furnished room in the largest house which he had ever entered. On his way thither he had caught the sound of many voices, laughing and talking, the tinkling of teacups, the scraping of a violin. Evidently some sort of a reception was in progress, for outside a canvas shelter was stretched to the curbstone, and a long row of automobiles and carriages was in evidence. It was almost ten minutes before the door was abruptly opened and Henriette Brinnen appeared. She had changed her clothes since luncheon, and was wearing a gown of some soft grey material, and a large hat with black feathers. In her hand she was carrying a small brown-paper package, sealed at both ends. The little smile with which she welcomed him was bewildering.

"I have kept you waiting," she exclaimed, "and I must send you away again quickly! Believe me, I am not always so inhospitable. This afternoon, as it happens, Madame is receiving and I must help her. I would ask you to come and be presented, but it is more important that you proceed swiftly with your mission."

"Of course," he assented, taking the parcel from her hand.

"Tell me first," she begged, keeping her fingers upon the closed door, "why were you so sad and silent all luncheon-time?"

He laughed a little hardly, hesitated, and was suddenly frank.

"Because," he told her, "I have not yet got used to my new role in life."

"But it is amusing, surely?"

"Perhaps I am old-fashioned," he sighed. "I rather resent being driven into the crooked ways."

"You are thinking only of yourself, then?"

"To be perfectly truthful," he assured her, "I was thinking very little of myself. I am afraid for you."

"But why for me?"

"Because you are reckless," he answered. "Your brother may be the cleverest adventurer who ever kept the police at arm's length, but there is always the risk. You cannot go on playing a part for ever. You may hide at the Milan

Court and call yourself what you will, and the chances are with you, but to borrow some one else's identity, to advertise yourself as the companion of a reigning princess, to occupy a position of trust and favour in her household and help to receive her guests, how long do you think that will go on?"

She laughed at him, but her eyes were full of kindness.

"You speak only of my brother's cleverness," she said. "Is that because I am a woman? Let me assure you, my dear friend, in many ways I am his equal. Your fears are exaggerated. I am right, am I not, when I assume that your present position is new to you?"

"It is," Aaron Rodd confessed. "Until these last few weeks—until the day, in fact, when I saw you first in the Embankment Gardens and Harvey Grimm sauntered, an hour later, into my office—I have lived miserably, perhaps, but honestly."

She laughed once more in his face.

"Oh, but you are so foolish!" she murmured. "Believe me, no person is really honest. We all live upon our neighbours. There is only one thing in life which is common to all religions—honour. By honour I mean fidelity to one's friends. Take that into your heart, dear Mr. Aaron Rodd, and you can hold your head as high as any man's on earth."

He stooped and kissed her fingers as she stood by the open door, an action, curiously enough, which he had never contemplated in his life before in connection with any woman, yet which seemed to him at that moment an entirely natural proceeding.

"That, at least," he promised, "is something which I can hold on to."

He descended the stairs, the clasp of her fingers still tingling on his, was handed from the grave major-domo, who guarded the hall, to another servant, and on to a footman, who summoned a taxicab for him. He gave the address of his office and was driven promptly off. A few yards from the corner of the Square, however, the taxicab slackened speed and stopped by the side of the pavement. Almost before he realised what was happening, the door was opened. An inspector, in uniform and peaked cap, let down the vacant seat and sat opposite to him. Mr. Paul Brodie, smoking a large cigar, followed and took the place by his side. The cab went on. Aaron Rodd remained stonily silent. The eyes of the two men were fixed upon the brown-paper parcel which he had had no time to conceal.

"Sorry to take you out of your way, Mr. Rodd," Brodie said, with ponderous sarcasm, "but we just want you to call for a moment at the Marlborough Street police station. In the meantime, you wouldn't care to tell us, I suppose, what you have in that small parcel you are holding so carefully?"

Aaron Rodd sat perfectly still. A chain of wild ideas flashed through his brain, only to be instantly dismissed. He thought of throwing the parcel out of the window, hurling himself upon the two men and making a fierce struggle for liberty. There was something ignominious in the facility of his capture, in the completeness of his failure. Yet he realised perfectly well that escape by any means was hopeless, that behaviour of any sort incompatible with his supposed position would be an instant confession of guilt.

"I am engaged on confidential business on behalf of a client," he announced stiffly, "and I cannot conceive what authority you have to delay me or to ask me questions."

Mr. Brodie nodded sympathetically.

"That's perfectly correct," he admitted, "perfectly correct."

Not another word was spoken until the cab drew up outside the police station. Mr. Brodie paid the taxicab driver, and Aaron Rodd, with an escort on either side of him, crossed the pavement, passed through the bare stone hall and into a small waiting-room. A superintendent, who was writing at a desk, glanced up as they entered. Mr. Brodie leaned down and said a few words in his ear. The former nodded and turned to Aaron Rodd.

"Have you any objection," he asked, "to our examining the parcel which you are carrying?"

"None whatever," Aaron Rodd answered coolly.

Mr. Brodie took it from him and carried it to the desk. The superintendent broke the seals and withdrew the lid from an oblong, wooden, jeweller's box. There was a mass of cotton-wool inside, which he hastily removed. Then his fingers suddenly stopped. He gazed downwards and frowned. Mr. Brodie's face was a study. The imprecations which broke from his lips were transatlantic and sufficing. Aaron Rodd, emboldened by their consternation, stepped forward and looked over their shoulders. At the bottom of the box reposed a small, black opal scarf-pin, the safety-chain of which was broken. The superintendent rose to his feet, whispered something sharply to Mr. Brodie, who lapsed into a gloomy silence, and turned to Aaron Rodd.

"Do you mind telling me where you were taking this box. Mr. Rodd?" he asked.

"To a jeweller's, to have the pin mended," was the prompt reply.

The superintendent replaced the wadding, thrust the lid back along its grooves, tied up the box and returned it to its owner.

"We are very sorry to have interfered with your mission," he said, "but before you leave us I am going to ask you, so that we may be perfectly satisfied, to allow me to search your person."

Aaron Rodd shrugged his shoulders.

"Pray do as you will," he consented, holding out his arms.

The superintendent went carefully through his pockets, felt his clothing and returned to his place.

"We are very sorry to have detained you, sir," he said—"the necessities of the law, you know. Inspector, get Mr. Rodd another taxicab."

"I know something about the law," Aaron Rodd declared, trying hard to feel that this was not some absurd nightmare, "and I still fail to realise on what possible authority you can practically arrest a solicitor leaving the house of an exceedingly distinguished client, break the seals of a private packet, and dismiss him without a word of explanation."

The superintendent glanced severely at Mr. Brodie.

"We are unfortunately in the position, Mr. Rodd," he confessed, "of having been misled by false information. We can do no more nor less than apologise. Our action, mistaken though it seems to have been, was undertaken in the interests of the law, with the profession of which you are connected. I hope, therefore, that you will be tolerant."

Aaron Rodd received his packet, wished the three men a brief "Good afternoon" and left the police station. He drove at once to his office, where he found the poet reclining on three chairs drawn up to the window, with a block of paper in his hand and a pipe in his mouth.

"Where's Harvey Grimm?" Aaron demanded.

The poet laid down his pencil and waved his hand.

"Gone!"

"Gone? Where?"

"I have no idea," was the bland reply. "I spent an hour or two at the Milan, conversing with several friends, and incidentally looking out for Mr. Brodie. Then an idea came to me. I needed space and solitude. I thought of your empty rooms and I hastened here. If you would like to listen—"

"Damn your poetry!" Aaron Rodd interrupted. "Tell me what you mean when you say that Harvey Grimm has gone? He was to have been waiting here for me."

"As I left the Milan," the poet explained. "I inquired of the hall-porter if Mr. Harvey Grimm had returned. The man told me that not only had he returned, but that he had left again in a taxicab a few minutes afterwards. I understood the fellow to say that he had gone into the country and would not be back for several days."

Aaron Rodd put his hand to his forehead. Already a dim suspicion of the truth was finding its way into his brain. Then there was a gentle tinkle from the bell of his newly installed telephone. He took up the receiver. The voice which spoke was the voice of Harvey Grimm.

"That you. Aaron?"

"Yes!"

"Anything happened?"

"Yes!"

"It's O.K. You needn't explain. Back in about a week. So long."

Aaron Rodd laid down the receiver. He was still a little bewildered, oppressed by a certain sense of humiliation. He threw the packet, which he had been carrying so carefully, upon his desk and scowled.

"What's upset you?" Cresswell asked amiably.

"Seems to me I'm nothing but a cat's-paw," Aaron Rodd replied gloomily. "A messenger boy could have done my job."

"Don't worry," the poet advised. "By the by, you don't happen to know of a rhyme for silken, do you?"

The telephone bell, ringing once more, intervened to save the poet from the ink-pot which Aaron's fingers were handling longingly.

"What is it?" he demanded, taking up the receiver.

"Just a little message for Mr. Aaron Rodd, please," was the soft reply. "Please forgive me—it was so necessary. And the pin was for you—a little peace-offering. Will you please have the chain mended and wear it."

That was all. There was no pause for any reply. The connection was finished. Aaron laid down the receiver, lit a cigarette, and almost swaggered back to his desk.

"Sorry, old fellow," he said genially. "I can't seem to think of one for the moment. I'll have a try."

CHAPTER IV

ULYSSES OF WAPPING

On the following morning. Aaron Rodd, somewhat to his surprise, received a visit from his only client Mr. Jacob Potts, who was a publican and retired pugilist, and whose appearance entirely coincided with his dual profession, looked around the apartment with a little sniff.

"Ho!" he exclaimed. "Better times arrived, eh? 'Ad a spring-cleaning, 'aven't you? Telephone, too, and new chairs! Golly! Does it run to cigars?"

Aaron Rodd shamelessly offered him a box of Harvey Grimm's Cabanas. His client bit off the end of one with relish and seemed inclined to swallow it. He eventually spat it out, however, lit the cigar, and, throwing himself back in a chair, crossed his rather pudgy legs.

"Know anything about maritime law?" he began.

"Not much," Aaron Rodd admitted. "A lawyer very seldom knows anything outside his little bent," he went on. "We have great rows of books properly indexed, turn up the point and read the decisions."

"Where are yourn?" Mr. Jacob Potts inquired, looking around the somewhat bare walls.

"Pawned," Aaron Rodd confessed. "All the same, I can get into the law library and give you an answer on any point you like to put forward, within a very few minutes."

Mr. Potts nodded.

"That's why I kind of took a fancy to you years ago, when you was a nipper," he confessed. "No doubling and twisting about you. Just a straightforward answer to a straightforward question. 'Do you know anything about maritime law?' sez I. 'No.' sea you, 'but I can find out.' And so you can. Now one of the regular kidney of you fellows'd have been messing about for half an hour and then have read it all out of a book. You never tumbled to it yet, guvnor, did you, what my new line of business was?".

"Never," Aaron Rodd acknowledged. "From your conversation at various times I gathered that you saved money in the ring, acquired a prosperous public-house property, and were in some way or other responsible for the organisation of labour in your neighbourhood."

Mr. Jacob Potts grinned.

"Let it go at that," he decided. "Well, the point I want to know about is this. Supposing in the course of business I committed an offence, against the law, you understand, and I legs it out for a nootral country, you see—might be Holland, for instance—can I be 'auled off a Dutch boat in nootral waters on my way to Holland?"

"It would depend," Aaron Rodd replied, "on the nature of your offence. I will let you know your exact position, if you like to come in a little later."

"That goes," Mr Potts agreed. "I've a call to make at a public-house in Craven Street. There's a promising lad there I saw with the gloves on for the first time in 'is life the other night. I thought of making a match with 'im against Canary Joe. 'Ave you ever seen Canary Joe box?"

"I have never seen a boxing match in my life," Aaron Rodd replied.

"Lumme!" Mr. Jacob Potts gasped. "Well, I suppose yours ain't a sporting profession. Mine is—in every sense of the word," he added with a grin. "What about twelve o'clock, guvnor? That'll give me time to get a can of beer and some bread and cheese."

"I shall be quite ready for you at that time," Aaron Rodd promised. The ex-publican departed, and Aaron Rodd, after giving him time to get away, followed him out into the street, spent half an hour in the nearest law library, and returned with a volume under his arm. He found the poet seated on the top of the stairs outside his rooms.

"My dear fellow," the latter exclaimed peevishly, as he rose to his feet, "this new habit of yours of locking the door after you is most inconvenient."

"Why not go to your club and wait?" Aaron Rodd suggested. "It's only a few yards away."

"Inhospitable," the other sighed, "and I have come to you filled with a most generous idea. Listen. This may seem a commonplace thing to you, but to me it is an epoch in my career. I have opened a banking account."

"I noticed that the book-shop was thronged, as usual, as I came by," Aaron Rodd remarked.

"This week," the poet declared solemnly, "will practically sever my connection with the book-shop. My publishers insist upon it that my work must be distributed in the regular fashion. Henceforth, the poems of Stephen Cresswell will be on sale at every reputable bookseller's—at four-and-sixpence, if you please. I have also an agent, and, as I before remarked, a banking account. Things have changed with me. Aaron Rodd. Only yesterday I found myself in need of a ten-pound note, referred the matter to my publishers and found them most affable…. How are adventures this morning?"

"Nothing doing," was the prompt reply, "until Harvey Grimm comes back. My only client has been to ask me a question about maritime law. He is coming back directly."

The poet ignored the hint.

"My presence here will do you good," he pointed out. "He will perhaps take me for another client. He is not a man of culture, by any chance?"

"He is not," Aaron Rodd admitted tersely, "nor is he one of those who have been whacked into reading your poems."

"He must have read about them, at any rate," Cresswell insisted a little irritably. "If you introduce me, you had better mention my identity. Fame so far has left me quite unspoiled. I still feel a little thrill of pleasure in noticing the effect which the mention of my name has upon strangers.... Come in," he added pleasantly, in response to a thunderous knock at the door.

The door opened and Mr. Jacob Potts entered, bringing with him a strong atmosphere of old ale and bread and cheese. To Aaron Rodd's surprise, he recognised the poet with a broad grin.

"My Ulysses of Wapping!" the latter exclaimed, holding out his hand. "What a meeting!"

Mr. Jacob Potts jerked his thumb towards Cresswell as he turned to the lawyer.

"One of my clients," he remarked.

Aaron Rodd was puzzled. He had once paid a visit to the riverside public-house over which Jacob Potts presided, and he found it hard to associate Cresswell in any way with the atmosphere there. Mr. Jacob Potts had pressed a thick forefinger to his lips.

"Mums the word, guvnor," he declared reassuringly. "Don't you worry."

The poet picked up his hat.

"From this gentleman," he asserted grandiloquently, "I have no secrets. To be frank with you, it was he and another friend who are responsible for those incidents in my career with which you have been professionally connected."

Mr. Jacob Potts glanced at him admiringly. "That's 'ow 'e talks down at Wapping. Ain't it wonderful?" he observed.

Stephen Cresswell edged towards the door. "When you have finished with our friend here," he said, addressing Aaron, "come across to the Milan. I have a proposition to make anent the opening of my banking account. It is connected with food and drink. Au revoir! Farewell, my riverside Goliath," he added, waving his hand to Jacob Potts. "Remember, our little bargain still goes."

Mr. Potts's large face was convulsed into humorous wrinkles.

"That's a queer gent," he declared as the door closed. "Come to me, 'e did, some time ago—heard I'd been a bit of a bruiser, and asked me to teach 'im a knockout blow, something quick and dangerous. Lord love me, I used to let 'im go on, and give 'im 'is fill o' beer, for the sake of hearing 'im talk! 'Ow I larfed when I tumbled to 'is game—me and the missis! He'd written some stuff wot no one would read, and 'is idea was to advertise it. Up you goes to an old gent at a dark corner. ''Ave you read my book?' he arsks. 'No!'

sez the old gent. 'Cresswell's Poems, eightpence a copy, number 32, Manchester Street,' he sez, and biffs 'im one. Then other nervous old gents 'ear about this and buys the poems, gives the proper answer when they're tackled, and 'ome they goes to tea. 'Oly Moses, it was a great scheme, but it was a greater before I'd done with it!"

"Where did you come in?" Aaron Rodd asked curiously.

Jacob Potts drew his chair a little closer to Aaron Rodd's desk.

"Well," he explained, "it's giving things away a bit, but to one's lawyer I don't know as it matters. I'm a kind o' provider of men as can be trusted to give anyone a clout on the side of the 'ead and no questions arst. I could lay my hand at the present moment on some fifty of 'em, good to give any ordinary person a doin'. Why, the third night after yon chap'd come to me, I'd twenty-five of 'em out, all asking the same question, at ten bob a time. It cost 'im a bit."

"But where on earth did he get the money?" Aaron Rodd asked. "He was broke when we met him first."

"I financed him," Jacob Potts confessed. "I tell you the idea fair tickled me. I found the coin and he paid me back like a gentleman. I only sends 'em out now when we're slack with other work, but whenever we 'ave a little affair doing, whatever the cost may be, we always commence it the same way—'Ave you read Stephen Cresswell's poems?' 'No.'—and then biff!"

The publican leaned back in his chair and his fat body shook with laughter. He mopped the tears from his eyes with a big red bandanna handkerchief.

"To think of meeting 'im 'ere!" he murmured weakly. "You see, we 'as our jokes even in the serious professions. Not that I ever let my boys go too far," he concluded, "and I keep 'em out of trouble as much as I can. That's why I want to know the law about this sea business."

Aaron Rodd read him extracts from the volume he had brought back, and explained several doubtful points. The publican's face was a little grave when he had finished.

"I ain't at all sure," he decided, "that I fancy trusting any of my best boys with this job, and I loathe foreigners anyway."

"Well, I won't ask you any questions," Aaron Rodd said, "but if you want any free advice, here it is. You've made plenty of money. I should keep friends with the law, if I were you. You can't employ such a band of ruffians as you've been talking about, and not find a wrong un amongst them now and then."

"If one o' my lads," Jacob Potts declared solemnly, "was to squeal, I tell you the rest would be on 'im like a pack of fox 'ounds on a fox. They'd tear 'im limb from limb, that's wot they'd do."

"That wouldn't do you a great deal of good if you were in prison," Aaron Rodd reminded him. "However, you know the law now."

"I know it, and I ain't sweet on the job," Mr. Jacob Potts confessed. "'Owsomever! Good-morning to you, Mr. Rodd, and much obliged. You'll add your little bit on to my quarterly account.... Wot 'o, another client!" he added. "I'm toddling."

He shook hands with his adviser and reached the door just as it was opened and Henriette entered. He stood for a moment, as though stupefied. Then, as he disappeared through the doorway, he turned round and winked solemnly at Aaron.

"Wishing you good morning, guvnor!" he said as he closed the door.

Curiously enough, as on that first morning when they had met in the Embankment Gardens, a little ray of wintry sunshine which had stolen in through the dusty, uncurtained windows lay between them. Aaron Rodd, whose first impulse had been one of joy at this unexpected visit, stopped suddenly in his progress across the room. There was something so entirely different about her, a change so absolute and mystifying. The faintly supercilious deportment and expression of the young woman of the world, carrying herself so easily and with such natural grace and self-possession, seemed to have deserted her. She was suddenly a frightened child seeking for shelter, and with a lightning-like effort of imagination he seemed to see her flying for sanctuary from those terrors of which he had already warned her.

"Is anything wrong?" he inquired quickly—"anything fresh. I mean?"

She sank into his chair. She was panting a little, as though she had been hurrying.

"I am afraid!" she confessed. "I am terrified! Give me your hand to hold, and listen."

She gripped his strong fingers. They both almost held their breaths. There was no sound except the distant rumble of traffic. By degrees she grew calmer.

"You are not worrying about my errand?" he asked anxiously. "You know what happened to me?"

"It isn't that," she told him simply. "That was all planned beforehand. You didn't mind?"

"Of course not," he assured her.

"It is something which happened before I came to England," she went on, "something terrible, something from which it seems to me I can never escape. Listen ... I must tell you one day—I shall tell you now. Leopold has always been fortunate, but the luck went against me one day. I was face to face with detection. I had the whole of the jewels in my possession. I was confronted with the worst. I hadn't time to think. I killed the man who would have brought ruin on all of us, and, on me, worse than ruin.... Do you hear?—I killed him!"

Aaron Rodd sat speechless. She seemed so small and delicate-looking. It was incredible!

"He was a great man—a colonel in the Prussian Guards. He had high connections, some of them Belgian. The threats of his people reached my ears even before I had escaped. They swore to get me back into Belgium, and if I were once there, God knows what would happen to me! At first, when I reached London, I felt safe. I managed to become attached to the household of Madame. Surely in London was sanctuary! And lately I have felt different. This man—I will not tell you his name—he is connected even with the family of Madame herself. I begin to fear that they have suspicions. The Princess has been cold to me lately. There are several others in the household who seem to look askance at me. I have had letters from relatives in Belgium, inviting me to go back. Some of them, I know, have been forgeries. During the last few days I have been followed about. Only yesterday there was a little fog. I was in the square, near the corner of Brook Street. Suddenly I heard swift footsteps just behind me, there was a whistle, a taxicab drove up by the kerb. There was a man in it, sitting back in the corner. I saw his face—it was cruel, horrible! I could hear another man running from out of the fog towards me. I knew what they wanted—to thrust me into the taxicab. And just at that moment I shrieked, and two strangers came from one of the big houses and I clung to them. The taxicab drove off and the man seemed to melt away. The two gentlemen thought I was mad. They escorted me to another taxicab. Since then I dare not move alone."

"How did you come here?" he asked. "In one of Madame's cars. It waits for me outside. Even at the corner of this street there were two men who frightened me. Today my week of service is up with Madame. She has not encouraged me to stay longer. She looks at me with the eyes of suspicion. And at the Milan Court I am afraid! My grandfather is so old—the world is finished for him. And Leopold is so cold and mysterious. He comes and goes with never a word. There! You see what has happened to me!" she exclaimed, with a little quaver in her tone. "I have lost my nerve. And I have been brave. Monsieur Aaron Rodd—believe me, I have been brave."

"Of course you have," he answered encouragingly, "and of course you will continue to be brave. You must not fancy things. Believe me, you are safe here—safe, at least, against being sent back to Belgium against your will. The fears I have for you and about you—"

"Well, what are they?" she interrupted anxiously. "Tell me about them."

"These diamonds," he continued slowly. "If I might venture to say so, it seems to me that your brother is making a mistake in dragging you into the affair at all. We could have done our business with him and left you out of it."

"But he is watched every hour of the day," she explained. "They cannot find the jewels, and they can prove nothing against him unless they do find them, but they know very well that soon he must dispose of them, and they never willingly let him out of their sight. Besides, we are all to share in the proceeds. Why should we not take a little of the risk? Oh, believe me," she went on eagerly, "I can face anything that comes to me through the jewels. It is the other thing I am afraid of. I cannot speak even to you of that awful moment. The man who guessed our secret—he offered silence. We were alone...."

She broke off suddenly, absolutely incapable of speech. She was white almost to the lips. Her eyes were filled with reminiscent horror. He leaned over and took her hands once more, a little clumsily, in his.

"Don't think of it," he begged. "That part of it, at any rate, is done with. One must fight for what one has, for the sake of others."

"I know—I know!" she agreed, trying to smile at him. "But tell me again—there isn't any way, is there, that the Belgian authorities—I suppose they do still control their own law-courts—could be cajoled into having me sent back? I am frightened. I begin to wonder whether these men, who I am sure have been watching me, are emissaries from the foreign police."

He smiled reassuringly.

"Not a chance," he declared. "They have something else to do just now. Believe me, you are frightening yourself about nothing. If you are being watched, and I should think it extremely probable that you are being watched, it is simply because you are living under the same roof as your brother and because you are an exceedingly likely medium for the disposal of the jewels."

"If I were sure that that was all!" she murmured.

"It is all," he told her confidently. "There! Besides, in that other case, remember that you are not friendless. I don't think I need tell you," he went on, a little awkwardly, "that if there were any way I could help, any way I could ensure your safety, it would make me very happy."

"I think that I felt that," she answered softly. "I think that that is why I came to you. Leopold has gone to one of his hiding-places—I do not know where—and he will not be back for several days. Please do not go far away. Be where I can telephone to you, or come."

"I wouldn't ask anything better," he promised.

Her eyes glowed for a moment. She gave him her hand impulsively, and he was dizzy with the strangeness and the joy of it. He had been so long debarred from intercourse with her sex that femininity was making a late but extraordinarily subtle appeal to him. He found himself, even in the moment when he was studying the colour of her eyes, counting the wasted years of his life, remembering with a sick regret the lines upon his face, the streak of grey in his hair.

"You are going back now to the Milan?" he inquired.

"From here. You could not—?"

"Of course I could," he assented eagerly, taking down his hat. "I promised to meet our friend Cresswell there."

"That ridiculous poet!" she laughed. "Whatever made him a friend of yours?

"He would tell you Fate," was the smiling reply. "Harvey Grimm would tell you a sense of humour. I really don't know what I could say about it. He isn't a bad fellow."

"You are sure you have no more business to attend to?" she asked earnestly. "I can sit and wait quite patiently while you finish."

He sighed as he closed his desk. "I am afraid my office itself is rather a farce," he told her. "As a lawyer I have been a failure. My only client passed you on the stairs as he went out."

She heard him a little incredulously.

"That seems so strange," she observed. "I am sure that you are clever."

"The majority of the world seems to have come to a different conclusion," he sighed, as he stood on one side to let her pass out.

"Here comes your client back again," she whispered. "I will wait for you upon the landing."

Mr. Jacob Potts came puffing up the stairs. He beckoned mysteriously to Aaron Rodd, and drew him on one side.

"Guvnor," he whispered, "'ave you got any pals in this building?

"I don't know that I have, particularly," was the somewhat doubtful reply. "Why?"

"Gave me quite a turn," Mr. Potts confessed. "There's two of my boys below, two of them who are on that job I came to consult you about."

"They are probably shadowing you," Aaron Rodd suggested.

"I'd give 'em shadow, if they tried that game on!" Mr. Jacob Potts asserted truculently. "'Owsomever, you've got the office, if there's any pals of yourn about. If you've any fancy, sir," he added, as he turned away, "for seeing a little bout tonight down at my place, I've arranged for that young fellow I spoke about to come down and put 'em on with Canary Joe. 'Arf-past nine, and no questions arst of a friend.

"I'll remember," the other promised.

"Won't keep you no longer," Mr. Potts observed, turning heavily away. "There's other clients than me about this morning, wot 'o!"

He turned back from the doorway and indulged in a huge and solemn wink.

"'Arf-past nine," he called out, "nothing charged for admission, but the salt air down Wapping way encourages the thirst, which is good for the trade. Bring a pal, if you've a mind."

Aaron waited until his client had reached the first landing before he rejoined Henriette. They drove in what was, to him, unaccustomed splendour to the Milan, and parted in the little hall.

"It is foolish," she said, as she held out her hand, "but I feel better because I have been frank with you. Sometimes my fears seem so unreal, and then sometimes I close my eyes and I get these horrible little mind-pictures. Ah, but you do not know the terror of them! This is England, though, and that was what they all said—'In England you will be safe.' Tell me you are sure that I am safe?"

"Absolutely," he declared confidently.

She waved her hand to him from the lift, and he proceeded to the smoking-room in search of Cresswell.

* * * *

The poet, having received forty pounds from his publishers, was thoroughly disposed towards a frivolous evening. He was consequently a little dismayed when, as they sat at dinner that same evening, Aaron Rodd, who had been a little distrait, suggested an alteration in their evening's entertainment.

"I wonder," he said, "if, instead of going to the Empire, you would care to see a bout between Canary Joe and a youthful barman who I understand possesses genius?"

The poet made a wry face.

"I am rather fed up with biffing just now," he confessed, "but Canary Joe—why, that's old man Potts's protégé."

Aaron nodded.

"The affair is to take place in a room at the back of his public-house," he observed.

Cresswell sipped his wine and considered. His attitude was obviously unfavourable.

"I am in the humour," he declared, "for a more enervating atmosphere, the warmth and comfort of the Empire lounge, the charm of feminine society—even from a distance," he added hastily. "I am feeling human tonight, Aaron Rodd—very human."

"It is possible," his companion continued slowly, "that an adventure—"

The poet's manner changed. "More than anything in the world I am in the humour for an adventure," he asserted eagerly.

"Then I think we will see Canary Joe," Aaron Rodd decided. "You shall be my guide."

The long taxi-ride would have been a little depressing but for the poet's uproarious spirits. He sang himself hoarse and filled the vehicle with cigarette smoke. They reached at last a region of small streets all running one way; in the background a vision of lights, suspended apparently from nowhere, the sound of an occasional siren, the constant, sometimes overpowering odour of riverside mud. When at last the taxicab came to a standstill, they were near enough to the river to hear its rise and fall against a little bank of shingle. From behind the closely drawn windows of the public-house, one side of which seemed to abut on to the riverside, came the sound of many voices.

They dismissed the taxicab and pushed open the swing-doors. The poet, who had been complaining bitterly of thirst on the way down, led the way to the counter. "Two whiskies and sodas, Tim," he ordered. "Where's the guvnor?"

The man jerked his thumb over his shoulder.

"Up in the room, getting things to rights," he announced. "If you take my advice, Mr. Cresswell, you'll slip in there as soon as you've had your drink. There'll be a crowd when the gong goes, and they're a tough lot to struggle with for seats."

Aaron glanced around. The room was filled with a motley throng of riverside loafers, with here and there a sprinkling of sailors. One huge Dutchman, in a soiled nautical uniform, was already furiously drunk. The two young men slipped up the stairs, to which the poet led the way, and passed through the door into the further apartment, just as the Dutchman's truculent eye fell upon them.

"Shouldn't wonder if we didn't tumble across something in the way of an adventure here," the poet remarked cheerfully. "We ought to have changed our clothes. Hello, here's the boss."

Mr. Jacob Potts, on his way down the long, dimly-lit room, came to a sudden standstill. His expression scarcely confirmed the welcome which the heartiness of his invitation earlier in the day had promised. He glanced at the two visitors in something like dismay. Nothing however, could damp the poet's spirits.

"We've come down to see the scrap, guvnor," he declared.

"If you have," Mr. Jacob Potts replied, with something which sounded threatening in his tone, "you're welcome. If so be that you've any other reason for your coming, maybe a word of advice from me wouldn't be out of place, and that word's git."

"When we've seen the scrap and not before," Cresswell chuckled. "Do you know that it cost the best part of a quid to get down here, guvnor? Bring 'em in and let's see what stuff they're made of."

Jacob Potts looked at the speaker doubtfully.

"You've 'ad a drop, young fellow, you 'ave," he muttered.

"Trenchantly and convincingly put, old chap," the poet replied, steadying himself by the back of a chair. "My dear friend and I are making an evening of it."

Mr. Potts's face cleared a little.

"Boys will be boys," he assented amiably, "and there's none of you the worse for a drop o' good liquor on board. Fact is I'm a bit jumpy tonight," he confessed. "My boys have got a little game on—tonight of all nights! Did you happen to notice," he asked anxiously, "if that goll-darned Dutchman was down there?"

"There is a son of Holland in the bar," the poet replied, "in a glorious state of inebriation. He is seeking for some one to destroy. Tell you the truth, we fled before him. His eye rested upon us and he scowled."

Mr. Jacob Potts lifted a blind and stared out towards the river.

"That's his steamer lying there," he muttered. "I wish to God he'd get aboard her!"

Aaron Rodd moved softly to his side.

"Is this little game you spoke of," he inquired, "—the game your boys have on tonight—the one which brought you up to consult me about maritime law this morning?"

"It is," Jacob Potts admitted, "and wot about it?"

Aaron Rodd shrugged his shoulders. Before he could reply, however, a gong sounded. The door of the room was thrown open and a surging mob from the bar streamed in.

"Front seats," yelled the poet, making a dive forward, but Aaron caught him firmly by the arm.

"Stephen," he whispered, "there's something up here tonight. We may have to come into it. Let's get seats by the door, where we can slip out quietly. I'm not joking."

Considering all things, Cresswell was wonderfully amenable. They stood on one side and let the crowd rush past them and eventually found two seats against the side wall, within a few yards of the door. Mr. Jacob Potts seemed for the moment to have forgotten their existence. He was standing in the middle of the little ring, which was roped off on a raised platform, stamping with his heel upon the floor. There were shrill whistles and cries of, "Order."

"Gents," Mr. Potts announced, "this is a light-weight scrap, twelve rounds, between our old friend Canary Joe and a youngster I found in Craven Street—Jimmy Dunks."

He pointed first towards a pimply-faced young man, with flaxen hair brushed smoothly down over his forehead, attired in scarlet knickerbockers and a pink vest, over which heterogeneous attire he had thrown a soiled, light-coloured ulster. His opponent wore a thin flannel vest, a pair of dilapidated golfing knickerbockers, and the remains of a dressing-gown. They both arose and made awkward salutations. Canary Joe was evidently the favourite, but Mr. Potts himself led the applause for his opponent.

"Fair play, gents," he begged. "This young 'un is a stranger, but from what I've seen of 'im I believe 'e's out to do 'is best, and we none of us can't do more."

There were a few more preliminaries and the two young men faced one another. They moved round for a moment like cats, amidst an almost breathless silence. Then there were one or two wild plunges, a little more cautious sparring, and a yell of applause as the young man in the golfing knickerbockers landed his right very near his opponent's mouth.

"Don't you treat 'im too light, Canary," they yelled from the back. "Keep your eye on 'is left."

There was a brief pause at the end of the first round. Canary Joe sat scowling at his opponent as he received the attentions of his second. The next round, although without decisive effect, was more vigorous; the third produced a black eye each. The audience settled down to enjoy itself. Suddenly the door at the back of the room was opened and from somewhere below came the sound of a gong struck three times. There were little murmurs of annoyance, disjointed oaths and growls from various quarters, but, without a single moment's hesitation, at least a score of the audience rose to their feet and made for the door. Aaron Rodd and his companion watched them as they slunk by. The poet was exceedingly interested.

"Some one's going to get a biffing tonight," he confided. "I wonder what it's all about."

Aaron acted on an inexplicable impulse. "Let's go and see," he suggested.

The poet rose at once to his feet. He was ready enough, if a trifle dubious.

"They won't want, us butting in," he remarked. "All the same, we might see a little of the fun. It will be more like the real thing than this."

They passed down the few stairs into the bar. Several of the men had paused for a drink, but others had already slunk out into the street. Following on the heels of the hindmost, Aaron Rodd and his companion found themselves almost swallowed up in a sudden fog which had rolled in from the river. From somewhere in the midst of the chaos they heard a quick, authoritative voice.

"Joe, you and half a dozen of you take the corners of the street. Hold up anything that tries to come down. Start a fight amongst yourselves if there are coppers about. You others come out on the wharf."

"That Dutchman's in this. Ill swear," the poet whispered. "Let's try and find our way down to the river. I know where the gate is."

Almost as he spoke, a heavy hand descended upon his shoulder, and a dark, evil face was thrust almost into his.

"Look here, guvnor," the man said, "you mayn't be after any 'arm down 'ere, but it's one o' them nights we don't need strangers around. You tumble? The old man's wolves are out and they've a nasty way of snapping anything that comes along."

"What's the game. Sid?" the poet asked engagingly. "We're only here for a bit of sport."

"Never you mind what the game is," was the terse reply. "You get back and watch those two chickens scratching one another's faces."

There was a moment's silence. Then from a few yards off came the sound of a slight moan, as from a person suffocating.

"What's that?" Aaron Rodd demanded sharply.

"Never you mind what it is," was the swift reply from their unseen adviser. "Take your carcasses inside, if you want to keep them whole."

He vanished in the fog. Aaron Rodd gripped his companion's arm.

"Stephen," he muttered, "that was a woman's voice!"

"Sounded like it," the poet assented. "Have you got your electric torch in your pocket?"

"Yes!"

They heard the rattle of a key in the gate which led out on to the wharf. For some time it refused to turn. Again they heard the moan, and Aaron's blood ran cold.

"I can't stand this, Stephen," he whispered hoarsely. "Come on."

"One moment," the poet answered. "They can't get the gate open. I don't believe the guvnor's on to this. Stay where you are for a minute."

He hurried back, tore up the stairs and into the dimly lit room, filled still with breathless expectancy. It was the end of another round, during which Canary Joe had obtained some slight advantage. The poet walked straight up the room, regardless of the growls which assailed him, and touched its presiding spirit upon the shoulder.

"Guvnor," he said, "you told me, when we had dealings, that you'd never taken on any job in which there was a woman to be harried."

"That's right, boy," Jacob Potts agreed.

"There's a woman in the game tonight, a woman who has been brought down here by some of your lot, and who is down there now, either drugged or half conscious. They are trying to get her on to the Dutchman's steamer."

"How do you know it's a woman?" was the brief demand.

"I tell you we both heard her groan," the poet insisted.

Jacob Potts rose to his feet.

"Boys," he said, addressing the belligerents, "and gents, there will be a ten minutes' interval. Sorry, but it's business. Joe will serve the drinks, which for this occasion only will be free."

The ten minutes' interval, softened by the promise of free drinks, displeased no one. Jacob Potts, still in his shirt-sleeves, strode out of the place, through the front room of the public-house and out into the street, where a queer, unnatural silence seemed to reign.

"There ain't no woman about 'ere!" he exclaimed.

Aaron Rodd suddenly flashed his torch. The iron gate was closed. There was no one before it. They could hear the sound of men's footsteps a few yards away on the old wooden wharf.

"They've just gone through," Aaron whispered fiercely. "Come on!"

Jacob Potts produced a key from his pocket and swung the gate open.

"If you fellows have made a fool of me," he muttered, "there'll be trouble; but if my boys have let me in, there'll be hell!"

Just as he finished speaking they once more heard the faint, smothered cry from in front, followed by a man's oath. They saw the flashing of a light and heard the fall of a rope from the wharf into the river. Jacob Potts quickened his pace.

"Turn on that glim o' yours, guvnor," he growled, "and mind where you're going. 'Ullo there?"

There was a confusion of answering voices.

"It's the guvnor!" they heard some one say.

Then the light of Aaron Rodd's torch flashed upon the short, wooden dock, and upon the half-dozen men grouped at the top of the crazy steps at its furthest extremity. One of them came back. It was the man who had warned the poet and Aaron.

"Guvnor," he said earnestly, "this ain't your show. You leave us alone and get back to the fight."

"That be damned!" Jacob Potts replied firmly. "It's no job of yourn to tell me wot to do. You know very well there's just one thing I stick at, and I asks you a plain question, Sid, and a plain answer expected. Is that bundle you're carrying a woman, or ain't it?"

"It's a woman," the man proclaimed doggedly, "and it's going on board the *Amsterdam*."

The answer of Jacob Potts was bellicose and unprintable. He strode along the little wharf, followed by Aaron Rodd and Cresswell. Behind came the man called Sid, his face darker and more evil than ever, his breath coming short with anger.

"Boys," Jacob Potts exclaimed, "drop that! You hear me? Women ain't in the game. You've all been told that."

There was a moment's hesitation. Then they heard the voice of their leader, hoarse and vicious.

"Get on with it, boys. It's going to be the river for anyone who stands in our way tonight."

There were six of them altogether, besides Sid. Three of them moved now towards the steps, below which a boat was bobbing up and down. Another man was seated in it, holding to the side by a boat-hook, and the three men at the top of the steps were carrying something. Sid and the other two turned round.

"Guvnor—" the former began.

There was a sickening crash as Jacob Potts's fist caught him almost in the mouth. He rolled over and up again on to his feet, remaining warily out of reach, but after that one blow easily able to keep his assailant occupied. Aaron Rodd had sprung for the steps, and received a blow on the side of the head from one of the other men which sent him reeling almost into the river.

"Get her aboard," Sid cried out. "We can tackle this lot. No one can get down the street. The boys'll see to that."

Then there was a fierce, ugly silence for several moments. Jacob Potts, winded from the first, the river on either side of him and murder in the man's face whom he fought, panted and groaned with every fresh movement. Aaron Rodd found himself suddenly in a new world, a new uplifting instinct sending the blood tingling through his veins. He was fighting, a thing he had never done since his school-days, fighting with long, swinging blows, making scarcely an effort to protect himself, fighting in an atmosphere indescribable, the thirst for blood hot in his veins, with one desire throbbing in his heart—to kill or throw into the river the man who kept surging up towards him. It was a vicious face, fair-complexioned once but dark now with engine grease, with bleary eyes, mouth wide-open all the time, disclosing a broken row of hideous, sickly-looking teeth. But for the man's evil life he would have disposed of his opponent with his first few blows, for he had been in his day a bruiser of some repute, but Aaron Rodd knew no pain, felt no fear, and he was the first conqueror, through sheer fortune, hitting wildly with all his strength, his long right arm landed full on the point of his assailant's jaw. The man went over with a sickening crash. Sid, who was still sparring with Jacob Potts, leaned for a moment downwards.

"Lay her down in the boat and come up, one of you," he shouted. "Bill's done in. Get down and let the other boys through. They're at the gate. We'll finish off these blighters then."

One of the men who had been stepping into the boat, turned back. Suddenly there was a scream from below and Aaron Rodd knew that his had been no dream. The voice was Henriette's.

"Help! Help!" she cried.

Her voice was smothered, but Aaron Rodd's shout rang through the night.

"We're here, Henriette! We'll rescue you. Hold on."

Then there was the sound of a mighty splash. The poet, who had suddenly closed with his man, had got him to the very edge of the wharf. Apparently one or both had lost their balance. For a moment the fighting ceased. Every one listened. A few yards away they could hear the long, level strokes of a man swimming—one man only. Then Jacob Potts's voice broke the tense silence.

"I'm—I'm done," he moaned.

Aaron Rodd, who had been waiting for the two men running up the steps, swung round. A peaceful man all his life, he was suddenly a fiend. He seized the electric torch from his pocket and brought it down with all his strength on the head of Jacob Potts's opponent. The man fell over with scarcely a cry, just as the publican reeled backwards. The realisation of what had happened gave him a moment's extra strength.

"You've done him, sir," he faltered. "Can you keep those other two off for a moment whilst I get my wind? That brute—hit me—below the belt. I forgot he wouldn't fight fair. Mind this little one. He'll trip you."

Aaron Rodd turned almost with a laugh to meet his two assailants. It seemed to him that there was a new joy in the world. He whirled the torch over his head, missed the skull of the nearest of the newcomers and brought it crashing on to his shoulder. At the same time he himself received a fierce blow from the second man, staggered, tripped, and recovered himself. The whole place went round. He put his hands up for a moment before his head, felt them battered down, struck wildly again and again. One of his blows went home with a sickening thud, and the joy of it thrilled him. Both men were closing in upon him, however. On the other side of the wharf they could hear the gate being rattled. There was a low whistle, twice repeated. The man from the boat shouted. "Climb the gate, boys."

"There's more of 'em," Jacob Potts gasped. "Keep it up for a moment, Mr. Rodd. I'm coming in to help you."

Then there was another hush, ominous, in a sense mysterious. There was a sound which conveyed little enough to Aaron Rodd, but which the others recognised promptly enough—the long, mechanical swing of oars. Without a second's hesitation, Aaron's two assailants turned and ran, fleet-footed and silent, off the wharf, and vanished somewhere in the darkness. The gate was rattled no more and from up the street came the sound of flying footsteps. Jacob Potts began to sob.

"It's the police—the river police! That ever I should be glad to welcome 'em! Get down to the boat, Mr. Rodd. My God, what's come to you, sir!"

Aaron Rodd walked from one side of the quay to the other like a drunken man. There were all manner of stars in front of him. He gripped hold of the rope and stole down the steps. He was suddenly steadied by a great excitement. With a black shawl torn back from her head in that last struggle, her feet and hands tied together, the remains of a gag hanging from her mouth, her face livid, her eyes full of horrible fear, lay Henriette. She saw him swaying over her, gripping the end of the rope, his face streaming with blood, but with all manner of things in his eyes, and she made a little movement, tried to hold up her hands, tried even to smile.

"Oh, thank God! Thank God!"

The sound of the oars was no longer audible. A long boat, crowded with men in dark uniform, came gliding out of the shadows. A boat-hook gripped the side of the quay. The poet, looking like a drowned retriever, stood up in the bows and cheered lustily. One of the uniformed men, who seemed to be an inspector, flashed a lantern upon the scene.

"What's wrong here?" he asked quickly.

Aaron Rodd kneeled upon the slippery steps and pointed to the girl. One of the men clambered into the boat and cut the ropes. They half carried her up on to the wharf. The policemen followed. They flashed lanterns around. The man Sid was lying on his side, motionless, Aaron Rodd's first assailant was lying in a doubled-up heap, moaning to himself. Mr. Jacob Potts was just beginning to recover himself.

"So you're in this, are you, Potts?" the inspector remarked grimly. "The boys broken loose, eh?"

"Just a little scrap," the publican groaned.

Then Aaron Rodd was suddenly aware of a new sensation. He felt a pair of warm arms thrown around his neck. The poet, who had been shaking himself like a dripping dog, sprang to his side. The sky came down and the planks beneath his feet seemed jumping towards his throat. But Aaron Rodd, though the world around him was fading fast from his consciousness, had found new things and he was quite happy.

CHAPTER V

THE MYSTERIOUS ASSISTANT

Abraham Letchowiski stood in the doorway of his small but brilliant-ly-lit shop in one of the broad thoroughfares leading out of the Mile End Road and beamed upon the Saturday-night passers-by. He was, in his way, a picturesque-looking object—patriarchal, almost biblical. He wore a long, rusty-black frock coat, from which the buttons had long since departed, but which hung in straight lines about his tall, spare form. His dishevelled grey beard reached to the third button of his waistcoat. His horn-rimmed spectacles were pushed back to his forehead. Every now and then he harangued a likely-looking couple in mild and persuasive accents.

"Young shentleman, shtop von minute. Bring the beautiful young lady inside. I am selling sheap tonight—very, very sheap. Young shentleman, you want a real diamond ring? I have the sheapest diamond rings in the vorld. I am Letchowiski, the gem merchant. You bring your moneysh to me. You get better value than anyvere in Vitechapel or the Vest End. Come inside, my tears."

A few of the passers-by answered him with chaff. One or two of the more forward of the girls threw him a kiss. Old father Letchowiski on a Saturday night was a familiar feature of the dingy marketing thoroughfare, but tonight more than one fancied that his heart was not in it. Presently, during a lull, he turned back into his shop, fingered lovingly a few of his wares, gewgaws of the most glaring description, and then turned to a small boy who stood behind the counter, a remarkable, crosseyed youth, standing little higher than the counter, with black hair, a narrow face, and sallow complexion.

"David, you call me the moment anyone puts their head in the shop? You hear? Call loudly."

"All right, granfer," the boy replied. "Can I go to the door and snout at them?"

"If you like," the old gentleman agreed tolerantly. "If you sell anything, perhaps I give you a little commission."

A beatific smile spread over the boy's face as he scrambled under the counter.

Abraham Letchowiski opened a door which led into the rear of the premises, drew aside the curtain and peered for a moment back again through the shop into the street, over the head of the small boy, who with outstretched hands was making the night hideous with cries of fervid invitation. Then he dropped the curtain, descended two stairs, passed through a small, ill-ventilated sitting-room, the table of which was laid for a homely meal, on through another door, and along a dark passage. Through a further door at the end came a chink of brilliant light. He knocked twice softly and stepped inside. A man with a tired, livid face, his clothing covered by a long smock, heavy spectacles disfiguring his features, was stooping over a tiny lathe. The soft whirr of a dynamo from a corner purred insistently. A brilliant drop-light from the ceiling was lowered almost over the bench. Something glittered in the white hands of the workman as he turned around with a little start.

"Letchowiski!" he muttered. "Well?"

"Finish for tonight," Letchowiski whispered imploringly. "All the evening I have been uneasy. Just now I stand in my doorway and I shout my wares and my eyes search. There is a man in the clothing shop opposite. He pretends to deal with Hyam for a suit, but I see him often with his eyes turned this way. He is like the man of whom you have told me—the man Brodie."

The artificer did not hesitate for a moment. He looked in the mirror opposite to him and straightened a little more naturally the coal-black hair which only an artist could have arranged. With his foot he stopped the dynamo. From a cupboard opposite to him he brought out a dozen cheap watches and spread them around. One of these he proceeded with neat fingers to take to pieces.

"It is well to be careful. Abraham Letchowiski," he agreed softly. "Go back to the shop. Is supper ready?"

"There is a tittle cold fish upon the table," Letchowiski replied. "It is useless to wait for Rosa. We will sit down, you and I, when yon wish."

A faint flicker of disgust crossed the face of the listener. He watched the disappearing figure of the old man. Then he half closed his eyes.

"It is the end," he reminded himself softly. "All that remains is to get away."

Mr. Harvey Grimm took off his overalls and looked at himself carefully in the glass. He was wearing a well-worn blue serge suit, a flannel shirt and collar, a faded wisp of blue tie. His black hair was plastered down on to his forehead, ending on one side in a little curl, after the fashion of the neighbourhood. The man was so consummate an actor that his very cast of features seemed to have assumed a Semitic aspect. He readjusted his spectacles, busied himself at the bench for a few more minutes, covered over the dynamo, and finally made his way stealthily into the shop. He paused for a moment with his hand upon the counter, listening to the old man, who stood in the doorway. His fingers played with a tray of atrocious-looking pieces of cut-glass, set in common brass. Abraham Letchowiski, in one of his pauses for breath, glanced around and saw him.

"You have finished?" he asked eagerly.

"Finished," was the quiet reply. "Let us eat together."

The jeweller abandoned his place, which was promptly taken by the small boy.

"You go and have your supper, granfer," he begged. "I do some good business."

"Aren't you hungry?" the old man asked affectionately.

The small boy shook his head.

"I rather stay here and do business," he declared. "Young shentleman went by just now wants diamond ring to give to the lady. He promised to come back."

They left him standing upon the threshold, eager and expectant, and took their places in the musty little room before the fragment of cold fish, at which Harvey Grimm glanced for a moment in disgust. They had barely settled down before the door was thrown vigorously open. A tall, dark young woman, dressed in all the finery of the neighbourhood, swung into the room. She held out her cheek to her grandfather, but her bold black eyes rested upon Harvey Grimm.

"What a supper!" she exclaimed scornfully. "And after I've been away for nearly ten days, too! You don't expect me to eat this, do you?"

"Sit down, my dear, and take a little," the old man begged nervously. "If I had been sure that you had been coming—but we are never sure of you, Rosa. We expected you last Saturday, but you never came."

"Pooh! that Is your own lookout," the girl declared. "You are rolling in money, grandfather, and you live like a pauper. I wonder your young men stay," she added, showing a row of white teeth as she: beamed upon Harvey Grimm. "I'm sure I shouldn't, unless you treated me better than this."

"If you like, my dear," Abraham Letchowiski suggested, "I will go out and buy some fruit."

She pushed him back in his place.

"Sit still," she ordered. "I will eat with you what there is. Afterwards we will see."

They proceeded with their very scanty meal. The girl talked loudly about her situation in the great tailoring establishment, dwelt on the fact that she had just been made forewoman over one of the departments, invited their admiration of the cut of her skirt, standing boldly up, with her arms akimbo, to display the better the allurements of her luxurious figure, her eyes flashing provocatively the whole of the time. Harvey Grimm, who had been at first silent and unresponsive, seemed suddenly to fall a victim to her charms. He met her more than half-way in the flirtation which she so obviously desired. They were seated arm in arm, whispering together, his lips very close to her flushed cheek, when the little door leading to the shop was suddenly opened.

Paul Brodie stood there, looking down upon them, and behind him another man, also in plain clothes.

There was a brief and somewhat curious silence. The two newcomers seemed content with a close scrutiny of the dingy, odoriferous apartment. It was Abraham Letchowiski who first spoke. He rose to his feet and leaned over the table. The hand which lowered his spectacles on to his nose was shaking.

"Vat you vant here?" he demanded.

"Sorry to disturb you, sir," Brodie said pleasantly, bowing towards Rosa. "We want to search your premises. Don't be alarmed. Unless you have something to conceal we shall do you no harm, and we'll take care of all your treasures."

"But who are you, then?" the old man persisted—"Vy should you search my premises? I have done nothing wrong. I have lived honest always."

"That's all right," Brodie declared soothingly. "We ain't going to hurt you any."

"You know me, Mr. Letchowiski," the other man observed. "My name's Bone—John Bone. I am the detective attached to the police station around the corner. We won't worry you any more than we're obliged to, but on this gentleman's information we are bound just to have a look round."

"But my pizness—it will be ruined!" Abraham Letchowiski cried, wringing his hands. "If my customers know, they will never believe again that I am an honest man. I shall be ruined! They will come no more near my shop!"

"Nothing of the sort," the detective assured him. "I have only left one man outside and he is in plain clothes. We can search this room and the bedroom and your workshop, without attracting anyone's attention. Come, Mr. Letchowiski, you and I know one another."

The old man was still vociferous in his expressions of dismay.

"I am seventy-three years old," he moaned. "I have never been in trouble. I am honest, just as honest as a man can be."

"Then keep your hands exactly as they are now," Brodie told him. "So!"

With the ease of experience he ran his fingers over the old man's clothing, searching him from head to foot.

"Well, I never!" Rosa exclaimed, her eyes flashing angrily. "Fancy treating an old man like that! Is anyone going to try to do it to me, I should like to know? They'll feel my fingernails if they do."

"It will not be necessary," John Bone replied politely. "We watched you enter."

"What you looking for?" she asked, her curiosity getting the better of her anger.

"Ah!" the detective murmured, "Is this your assistant, Mr. Letchowiski?" he went on.

Harvey Grimm rose slowly to his feet and held out his hands.

"I am not an assistant of anybody's," he declared, and his voice seemed to have undergone an extraordinary change. "My name is Ed Levy, and I am a skilled watchmaker."

John Bone searched him briefly from head to foot. All the while, Brodie was going round the apartment. Cupboards were peered into, ornaments turned upside down, and boards and walls tapped, every possible hiding-place ransacked. John Bone disappeared for a few minutes up the stairs, and they heard his heavy tramp in the bedroom above. As soon as he had returned, the two men made their way towards the inner door.

"Come with us down to the workshop, Abraham Letchowiski," the detective invited.

"Vot you want me for?" the old man asked querulously.

"Never mind. Come along with us. We may have questions to ask."

They disappeared, the old jeweller groaning in the rear. As they passed through the door, Paul Brodie glanced for a moment back. The young man who had called himself Ed Levy had passed his arm once more through Rosa's. Their faces were close together. An amorous grin had parted the young man's lips and he was whispering in the girl's ear. Brodie smiled at his half-conceived suspicion, as he turned away. Rosa and her grandfather's assistant were left alone.

"What you think?" she asked him. "Has grandfather been doing anything, eh?"

"Not he," was the confident reply. "Abraham Letchowiski is too old and too clever to run such rusks at his time of life. Besides, he has plenty of money."

Rosa assented. She was apparently convinced of her grandfather's probity.

"You're right," she declared. "He has got plenty of money, and no one to leave it to except David and me. A nice dowry for me, eh?"

"Lucky girl!" Harvey Grimm sighed.

"These young men—they know it," she went on. "There's Mr. Hyam, from opposite, and the two Solomons. But I don't like them—they're too clumsy. I like you."

He held her hand tighter. She presented for his examination her fingers, exposing a very large and brilliant ring and a massive gold bracelet.

"I love jewellery," she confided. "Isn't that beautiful? Some day you give me a ring, eh, and I wear it—which finger you like me to wear it on?"

"Some day," he promised. "When I am earning a little more, I will give you a jewel that will make all the girls in your workshop mad with envy."

"If you want to earn more money," she asked, "why do you work for grandfather? All the young men make jokes about him. He never pays any one half what they are worth."

Harvey Grimm nodded mysteriously.

"You wait," he told her. "I never stay long anywhere. I am a journeyman repairer. I earn more money that way. I have about finished here now."

"Tonight," the girl whispered, "you take me to a cinema palace. There's a fine one at the corner of the street. If you like," she added with assign, "I pay for my own seat."

He hesitated for a moment. Then he smiled.

"We will start directly these men have gone," he promised. "And I will pay for both.

"That is better," she acquiesced, with an air of relief. "It is always better for the gentleman to pay. Tell me," she went on, a little abruptly, "what do they look for, these men? They are a long time in the workshop."

"It is always the same," he told her. "Wherever I go, I find it. There are always robberies, day by day, up in the West End, and they think there is nowhere else the stones can be brought and sold but in this neighbourhood. Every little jeweller's, shop from here to the far end of the Mile End Road is ransacked. This is the second time they have visited us."

"Then they are very foolish people," Rosa declared. "Grandfather wouldn't buy anything that was stolen. He is too nervous. He has no courage. Yet," she went on thoughtfully, "if he is really as rich as they say he is, one wonders how he makes it all out of this poky little shop."

Harvey Grimm nodded his head many times in wise fashion.

"A very clever man, Abraham Letchowiski," he declared. "Oh, I know many things! Those brooches he sells hundreds of at a shilling each—they cost one halfpenny. The engagement rings with the rubies or sapphires—you take your choice—nine shillings he charges for those, ten-pence halfpenny they cost him. Money comes soon when one can persuade people to buy. Then he lends money everywhere, when it is safe. Many of these tradespeople in the street owe him money.... Hush! They are coming back. After the cinema, perhaps we have a little supper together, eh?"

She hugged his arm affectionately, which was precisely what he meant her to do. The entrance of the three men found them engaged in amorous whisperings. Brodie scarcely glanced in their direction. He was frowning sullenly.

"Just a few minutes in the shop, Mr. Letchowiski," the detective said, "and we'll move on and leave you in peace."

They passed up the two steps and through the little door, which they closed behind them. Harvey Grimm for a moment seemed to forget his companion. He rose to his feet and stealthily crept to the curtained window. He stood there, peering through a chink into the shop. It was becoming difficult now to retain that wonderful composure. The hand which had stolen into his trousers pocket was tightly clenched upon a small, hard object.

"Why do you watch there?" Rosa demanded petulantly. "Come back to me. Grandfather will be here directly."

Her new admirer made no reply. His eyes were riveted upon Paul Brodie, who held in his hands the little tray, piled with abominable gewgaws. Presently he set it down again upon the counter. Harvey Grimm bit his lip until the blood came.

"Why do you bother about those stupid men?" she protested. "Come back here or I shall come to you."

He heard her rise with a great rustle. He felt the odour of patchouli and cheap sachets about him. She crept to his side just as the shop-door opened and the two men went out. Then he turned and kissed her full on the red, pouting lips. She giggled hysterically, for her grandfather had just pushed open the curtained door and was standing looking down upon them. He stamped his foot, shook his head, and raised his hands.

"You kiss my granddaughter—you?" he cried.

Harvey Grimm held out his finger. The old man suddenly stopped. He crossed the room towards his high-backed chair and sank back with a little sigh of relief.

"I am too old for excitement like this," he mumbled—"I am getting very old."

Rosa turned towards him.

"Mr. Levy is going to take me to a picture palace, grandfather," she announced. "Would you like me to call and ask Mr. Hyam to come across and sit with you?"

The old man shook his head.

"No, no!" he replied. "It would mean coffee for two and I have no money. You go to the cinema with Mr. Levy and enjoy yourself, my dear. These men have terrified me. I am old—too old. I shall go to Deucher's and get some coffee by myself. Come and get your supper," he cried through the open door to the boy. "I will come into the shop for a little time."

The boy came reluctantly from behind the counter and pushed past his cousin and her escort into the sitting-room. Rosa turned back to speak to him for a minute, and Harvey Grimm was alone in the shop. He stretched out his hand towards the tray of gewgaws, and a little shower of its contents slipped into his overcoat pocket. Presently Rosa reappeared, drawing on her gloves.

"We go now," she declared. "Walk slowly out of the shop. I like Mr. Hyam to see us, from opposite. He is always bothering me to go out with him. I like you best. There! This way."

They made a very deliberate progress along the crowded street until they reached the cinema palace. Harvey Grimm paid for sixpenny seats, and sat arm in arm with Rosa in an atmosphere which seemed to reek of fried fish, rank tobacco smoke, and cheap scent. His left hand held her purposely ungloved fingers inside her muff. His right hand toyed with forty thousand pounds' worth of diamonds, thrust into common settings which sometimes pricked his fingers. When the performance was over they left, still arm in arm.

"Rosa," he announced, "tonight I give you a treat. I tell you a secret as well. I am leaving your grandfather's. I have a much better place. I have saved money, too."

She clung to him in unrestrained affection.

"How much?" she whispered.

"Never mind," he replied. "Maybe three hundred pounds, maybe more. Tonight I have the spending fit upon me. We take a taxicab and we drive together up West. I give you some supper at the Monico."

She drew a little breath of delight. Suddenly she was serious.

"Let us go by the Tube," she suggested. "We shall save three shillings towards the supper. You can buy me a bottle of scent with that."

He laughed and handed her into the taxicab which he had already hailed, directed the man to drive to the Monico and stepped in by her side.

"I can buy you a bottle of scent all right," he assured her. "And in here, don't you see, we are quite alone, Rosa. In the restaurant there will be people."

"We might have had the taxicab home," she sighed, her head upon his shoulder.

"Listen," he explained. "After supper I pay for your taxicab, if you will, but I must leave you. I have to see a man on business at half-past eleven. It is my new employer."

For a moment she drew away and looked at him doubtfully.

"On business at half-past eleven?" she repeated. "What is your business? Are you an honest man, Ed Levy, eh?"

"I am as honest as your grandfather," he answered. "And listen, I am clever. I can make money—make it quickly."

She sat a little closer to him and with her own fingers drew his arm around her waist.

"Shall we be married soon?" she whispered. "Grandfather must die some day soon and there's no one knows how much money he's got. David and I will have it all."

"We'll talk about that," Harvey Grimm promised.

* * * *

At a few minutes after twelve on the following morning, Harvey Grimm, very spruce and very debonair, pushed open the swing-doors of the small smoking-room of the Milan and crossed the room with the obvious intention of proceeding towards the bar. A little welcoming chorus assailed him from a circular lounge in the right-hand corner of the room. Seated there were four of his friends whom at first he scarcely recognised. There was Aaron Rodd with his arm in a sling, a piece of sticking-plaster on his forehead, and a thick stick by his side; the poet, with a bandaged head and a shade over his eye; Henriette, looking a little fragile but very animated; and her brother, still in uniform, leaning back in an easy-chair by her side. Harvey Grimm stared at them all in blank and ever-increasing astonishment.

"Has there been an earthquake?" he asked, as he shook hands and exchanged greetings with everybody, "or have I, in my country seclusion, missed a scrap?"

"You have missed the scrap of your life," Cresswell replied eagerly. "You have saved your skin at the expense of untold glory."

"Tell me about it," the newcomer begged, as he took his place in the little circle.

"Where can one find words?" the poet began expansively. "It was an Homeric sight, a battle royal! It took place in the darkness, upon a slippery wooden wharf, with the black waters of the river beneath, and murderous parasites assailing us on every side. It was an epic of biffing, the glorious triumph of the unfit over the riverside apache. And let me tell you this, my friend Harvey—for an untrained fighter the world doesn't hold a man who can hit so quickly and so hard as our newly-established hero, Mr. Aaron Rodd. I have decided that he has earned immortality. I am composing a poem which I shall dedicate to him."

"Could I hear what it was all about?" Harvey Grimm asked meekly.

"Me," Henriette sighed.

Then they told their story, all of them in turn, except Brinnen, supplying details. Towards the end, however, the poet took up the running and finished alone.

"His face," the latter declared, gripping Aaron Rodd by the arm, "was like a pastel in white chalk against the soft background of velvety blackness. Heaven lit the burning light in his eyes. The swing of his right arm was like the pendulum of fate—"

"Oh, keep this rot for the poem!" Aaron Rodd interrupted forcibly. "If you want to gas, what about your own swim to the river police station?"

"A series of truly Homeric episodes," the poet assented, with a gentle sigh. "My pen shall give them immortality. I shall not forget to allude to the part which I, too, played in this drama of fog and river. The water was very cold," he added, suddenly finishing his cocktail.

"And our friend from the country?" Brinnen asked quietly. "How has he fared?"

There was a breathless silence. Harvey Grimm nodded slightly. He glanced around the room, of which they were the only occupants. Both doors were closed.

"All is well," he announced softly. "I returned last night. The business is finished."

"How much?" Brinnen inquired eagerly.

"There will be forty-five thousand pounds. I could not draw it all last night, but it will be paid within a week. I have nine thousand with me. Six of that I will hand over at any moment you please."

"There is no one in the room," Brinnen murmured suggestively.

Harvey Grimm drew out a pocketbook, ran some notes through his fingers and passed them over to Brinnen. Once more the latter glanced around the room. Then with his left hand he produced from the pocket of his coat a necklace of brilliants, one of which, the centre one, seemed to shine with a faint, rosy light.

"Better see what you can do with that," he remarked, tossing it lightly across.

Harvey Grimm held the necklace for a moment in his fingers before he slipped it into the concealment of his pocket. During that moment he caught an impression of Henriette's eyes, full of amazement, fixed upon it. She turned towards her brother.

"Leopold," she exclaimed wonderingly, "I do not remember—"

He brushed her words aside.

"You have not seen all," he told her significantly.

Harvey Grimm rang the bell.

"I warn you," he said, "that it will be a few days before I can abandon civilisation again, even for a task like this."

Brinnen moved uneasily in his chair.

"It is work, this," he pointed out, "which carries with it a special urgency. Remember that its results will last for a lifetime."

"Quite true," was the somewhat grudging admission. "It also means great risks. I have been as near the end of things, within the last twenty-four hours, as I care to be."

The waiter appeared with a tray full of cocktails. Harvey Grimm accepted his and leaned back in his chair with a beatific aspect.

"This," he murmured, "is one of the decadent luxuries denied to me in my country seclusion. Like many other things in life, it is almost worth while to lose it for a time, for the sake—"

He broke off in his speech. They all leaned a little forward in their chairs. From a side door at the farther end of the apartment, leading to the private suites in the hotel, a lift man suddenly appeared, with a valet upon his heels. They crossed the room with almost feverish haste. They were obviously distressed. A small boy followed, a moment or two later, with face as pale as death. There was a confused murmur of voices just outside the glass door leading to the main portion of the hotel, and a moment afterwards they reappeared with the manager between them, all talking excitedly at the same time. Then the door opened once more and a woman, tall and dark, in a long dressing-gown of green silk, rushed in. She threw out her hands towards the manager.

"Send for the police!" she cried. "My husband—he is murdered!… and my jewels—they are all stolen! The police, do you hear?"

They all vanished through the distant door, the woman clinging to the manager's arm and talking excitedly all the time. The little party looked at one another.

"That was Madame de Borria, the wife of the South American millionaire," Harvey Grimm said slowly.

"The woman who wears the necklace with the rose diamond!" Henriette exclaimed breathlessly.

Then there was a queer, tense silence. Captain Brinnen lifted his glass to his lips and finished his cocktail.

"There is more than one rose diamond in the world," he observed coolly.

CHAPTER VI

PAUL BRODIE STRIKES

Mr. Jacob Potts, blowing very hard, and with his tongue protruding from the corner of his mouth, finished an elaborate signature, patted his waistcoat pocket, in which he had just deposited a cheque, laid down the pen, and, leaning back in his chair, crossed his legs. He was once more occupying the distinguished position of being Aaron Rodd's only client.

"I never thought to do it," he declared. "I never thought to part with 'The Sailor-boys' while I was, so to speak, in the prime of life. It's 'aving the lads turn agin me that's done it. It shows, Mr. Rodd," he added impressively, "what money will do in this world."

"Financially," Aaron Rodd reminded him, "you are independent, absolutely independent of work."

"I know, but what's a man to do?" Mr. Potts replied with a sigh. "There was plenty down there always to keep me occupied, and those lads—well, I could have sworn to them running straight till that blarsted Dutchman came along. I tell you, Mr. Rodd," he went on, "I've done some deals in my life, and I've been up against propositions where money didn't seem much object. I've 'ad jobs brought to me which I wouldn't allow my lads to tackle, where they, in a manner of speaking, thrust a blank cheque down under my nose, but I never in my born days knowed money chucked about like them as was at the back of that Dutchman was willing to chuck it about. Why, for an ordinary job, if my boys got a tenner apiece they thought themselves on velvet. From wot Tim, my barman, told me, and he generally noses out wot there is going abaht, there was two 'undred quid for each of those boys if they got the young woman on board. No wonder they were kind of off their chumps!"

"Where exactly did they mean to take her?" Aaron Rodd asked.

Mr. Jacob Potts grinned.

"I bet she knows, sir, and I should have thought she'd told you before this," he replied. "Give every man 'is due, I say, and for an amateur that 'ad no more idea than a babe unborn how to put up his dukes, I must say you did fairly let into 'em, Mr. Rodd. I never seed a man lose 'old of 'imself so, in a manner of speaking, and as for that young gent as writes poetry, why, I'd make a bruiser of 'im in six months. 'E don't seem to feel pain. And bein' as we're on the subject of that scrap, sir, are you above taking a word of advice from an old man?"

"I certainly am not," Aaron Rodd assured him.

"If I was you, I should go a bit quiet with the young lady and 'er friends," Jacob Potts said seriously. "I've nowt straightforward to tell agin 'em, and that's a fact, but a bit here and a bit there is good enough for a man with a level head. There's three or four of 'er kidney in this country, and, if I'm not greatly mistook, they're wrong 'uns."

"I can't think that the young lady comes altogether under that designation," Aaron Rodd protested stiffly. "At the same time. Mr. Potts, I must admit that her associations are mysterious."

"Steer clear of them, sir, and take an old man's advice," the ex-publican begged. "I've 'ad things 'inted to me about them that I shouldn't like altogether to put into words...."

Aaron Rodd saw his client out and found an old friend ascending the staircase. Harvey Grimm was whistling softly to himself, his hat was at its usual jaunty angle, his violets were as fresh as ever, his clothes as carefully brushed. Only his expression was different. He was almost serious. He took Aaron by the arm.

"Put on your hat, my friend," he said. "We will walk for a little time."

Aaron obeyed, and they made their way down to the Embankment Gardens.

"Listen," Harvey Grimm began, looking around to be sure that no passers-by were within hearing distance, "there is such a thing as tempting Fate a little too far. I think we have come to the point when we had better draw in."

"Explain yourself, please," his companion begged.

"During the last few weeks," Harvey Grimm proceeded. "I have broken up and cut into different shapes nearly a hundred thousand pounds' worth of diamonds. I have actually handled nearly eighty thousand pounds in money. You and I are fifteen thousand pounds each to the good. Our friends want to go on. Frankly. I've got the funks. I'd like to cry off for a time."

"That doesn't sound like you," Aaron remarked.

"Perhaps not," his friend admitted. "All the same, I've no fancy for thrusting my neck into the noose. Brodie doesn't even know it himself, but he was hot on the scent last time. He found out, somehow or other, the very house in which I was living. We were in the same room. He even had me searched. Once I saw him stare. I thought it was all up. Then his suspicion passed. It was just the way one of the Jewish girls down there had accepted me, which put him off, but I tell you, Aaron, it was touch and go. Then the diamonds themselves—there was a stroke of genius there of which I am proud. I hadn't long to do it either. Where do you think I hid them?"

"No idea."

"Of course you haven't! Listen. I had set them roughly in common brass fittings, like a pile of common brooches that were being sold, and I mixed them all up together, let them lie there on the counter of the little jeweller's shop where I have been doing my work and where I was hiding. Brodie took up some and let them fall through his fingers. I tell you that was the closest shave of my life!"

"I think we should be wise to drop it," Aaron declared earnestly. "We are off the rocks now. Harvey. I am content with what I've got."

"That's how I'm feeling," the other assented, "and yet there's this last necklace. It seems rather playing it low-down on Brinnen not to get rid of that for him. You see, unless it's broken up quickly, it's more dangerous stuff to handle than the others."

"Why?" Aaron demanded.

"Don't be foolish," Harvey Grimm admonished, a little impatiently. "There's the hotel where it was stolen, right in front of you. Here am I with the necklace, a hundred yards away. There's Brinnen on the same floor. There's Madame de Borria—why, it's a daredevil piece of work, anyway?"

"You don't mean that its Madame de Borria's necklace you've got?" Aaron Rodd groaned.

"Of course it is!" Harvey Grimm replied, a little testily. "You saw it yesterday, didn't you? There it is in my overcoat pocket, the pocket nearest you, at the present moment."

Aaron Rodd paused abruptly before a bench and sat down. It was quite close to where he had first seen Henriette.

"Look here," he said, "or God's sake, Harvey, jump into a taxi at Charing-Cross there and take the thing off somewhere."

"Take it off?" was the grim response. "I'd give a cool hundred to be rid of it at this minute. The trouble is that if I make a single move in the direction of any of my haunts, the whole thing will be blown upon."

"You mean that you are being followed?"

"Brodie hasn't been fifty yards away from me since nine o'clock," Harvey Grimm muttered. "Madame de Borria saw him yesterday, just after the theft, and he persuaded her to put the matter into his hands. See that window—the end one but three on the top storey but two?"

Aaron looked up to where the spotless white front of the Milan gleamed through the budding trees.

"I see it," he admitted.

"That is the window of Madame de Borria. Now count five windows to the left and one down—that is my room. Now up again, and two on to the right, and you come to the apartments of Captain Brinnen, known to Paul Brodie as the redoubtable Jeremiah Sands. When you add to these geographical coincidences the fact that the necklace is at the present moment in my pocket, and that I can't move a yard without being followed, you will understand that one needs all one's wits this morning. We are getting just a little near the bone."

"Nearer than you imagine, perhaps," Aaron Rodd whispered. "Here's Brodie."

Harvey Grimm was, for a moment, curiously still. His frame seemed to have stiffened into a sort of rigid attention. One felt that his brain was working with the same concentrated force. He neither moved nor looked in the direction which his companion indicated. Instead he leaned a little further back in the corner of the seat and lit a cigarette.

"One needs to remember," he murmured, "that it is really quite a long time since I have seen this unwelcome intruder upon our privacy."

Brodie came strolling along the asphalt walk, puffing out his checks and gazing about him, as though exercise and an interested contemplation of the river were the sole reason for his peregrinations. He appeared to recognise the two men only in the act of passing them. He at once stopped short and greeted them in his usual hearty fashion.

"Pleasant little spot, this, for an hour's recreation," he declared. "I was thinking about you, by the bye, Grimm, as I walked along."

"I am flattered," was the calm reply. "I should have thought that all your attention would have been engrossed upon the little affair over yonder. I understand that Madame de Borria has placed the recovery of her necklace in your hands. Quite a feather in your cap, my friend, if you succeed."

Brodie glanced casually at the block of buildings in front.

"Yes," he assented. "I have that on my mind, of course. By the bye, were you going back to your rooms, by any chance?"

"I was on my way there."

"Come, that's fortunate. With your permission, we will walk along together."

The two men rose and they all strolled along towards the hotel.

"Curiously enough," Brodie went on, "I was wondering whether I should be likely to run up against you today, Grimm. We wanted to ask your advice. Inspector Dishwater and I, about that little affair the night before last. You heard the particulars, I suppose?"

"I was in the smoking-room," Harvey Grimm admitted, "when Madame came running down in her dressing-gown. Naturally, we heard the story told a good many times."

"Just so! Madame, it seems," the detective continued, "heard nothing, knew nothing, until late in the morning, when her maid told her that the floor valet was unable to obtain admittance to her husband's room. She at once stepped through the communicating door and found him still unconscious, with the necklace missing."

"Has he recovered yet?" Harvey Grimm inquired. "Is he able to give any account of what happened?"

"I saw him for a few minutes last night," Brodie replied. "He seemed still very dazed and confused, but he talked quite coherently. His story is simple enough and doesn't help us much. He was fast asleep—he can't even say at what hour—when he was awakened by the thrusting of a gag into his mouth and a bandage over his eyes. He thought at first it was a nightmare, and he tried to spring out of bed. He was held down, however, quite firmly, and something placed under his nose which made him feel just as though, to use his own words, he was sinking back to sleep again. He remembers nothing more until the morning, when he was found by his wife. The moment they released the gag he was violently sick, and the room certainly smells ethery."

"What about the necklace?"

"Well, the necklace, for some reason or other, seems to have been kept in a tin dispatch-box in his room. It was locked, of course, but the keys were under his pillow, a fact which the thief, whoever it was, seems to have known. The box was simply opened and the necklace taken."

"It all sounds as though the thief must have been some one staying in the hotel," Aaron observed.

The detective smiled pleasantly upon him. They had left the Gardens now and were approaching the back entrance to the Milan.

"The legal mind, Mr. Rodd," he remarked,—"the legal mind. Yes, I may say that we have come to that conclusion ourselves, Ditchwater and I. Some one staying in the hotel, we think."

They passed through the mahogany doors and Brodie rang the bell for the lift.

"By the bye, Grimm," he suggested, "have you any objection—you have so often asked me to have a look at your rooms here?"

"Delighted, I'm sure," the other assented cheerfully. "We had better get out on the restaurant floor and take the lift on the other side of the café. I am afraid you won't see them at their best just now. I only returned yesterday from a week's absence."

"That so?" Brodie murmured. "Say, these little trips away from town are very pleasant! I don't seem to be able to get away from my work often enough. Not that I've been doing much good," he confessed dolefully, "during the last few months. Things have been going rather against me, Grimm. I've put in a lot of work and it don't seem to have panned out according to expectations."

"Too bad!" Harvey Grimm sympathised. "You're up against a genius, though, Brodie—there's no question about that."

Paul Brodie nodded solemnly.

"I tell you, sir," he declared, "that Jeremiah Sands is more than a genius. He has the devil's own luck, too, and I have come to the conclusion," he added, dropping his voice to a confidential undertone, "that the young lady is almost as clever as he is. I don't mind admitting," he went on, as they passed through the cafe and stood waiting for the other lift, "that at one time, Grimm, I was inclined to think that you'd put it over me—that little affair of the faked diamond, you know, when we tried to make a scoop in Mr. Rodd's office, I have changed my mind, though. Jerry Sands was too clever ever to walk into a trap like that, I guess I did you an injustice there, Grimm, and you, Mr. Rodd. Things have been a bit better with you lately, though, haven't they?" he wound up, a little abruptly.

Aaron Rodd raised his eyebrows. He had the air of one who considered the last remark impertinent.

"Have they?" he observed coolly.

"No business of mine, of course," Brodie went on. "Say, is this your floor, Grimm?"

The lift had come to a standstill and they stepped out.

"My rooms are this way," the latter announced.

The little party traversed a corridor, at the further end of which Harvey Grimm threw open a door, leading through a small entrance hall into an octagonal sitting-room, having a pleasant outlook upon the Thames. A man was standing with his back towards them, gazing out of the window. He turned around at their entrance.

"Ah, our friend Ditchwater!" Brodie murmured. "You know Inspector Ditchwater, don't you, Grimm?"

"I know him, certainly," Harvey Grimm replied, frowning, "but I can't imagine what the mischief he is doing in my rooms?"

"Perhaps I ought to have explained," the detective said apologetically. "We have taken the liberty, Grimm, of making a few slight investigations in your apartments."

"The devil you have!" their tenant exclaimed, gazing through the half-open door into the inner room. "Is that the reason why my bedroom seems all upside-down?"

"Probably," the detective admitted,—"quite probably. You see," he continued, "you are, in your way, my friend, an exceedingly interesting person to the police in this country, as you were at one time, I believe, to the police of New York. When a little affair such as we've been talking about happens only, as it were, a few yards away from your rooms, why, naturally, we've some interest in your doings."

"Have you anything against me?" Harvey Grimm asked quietly.

"A few questions," the other murmured. "See here, Grimm," he went on, with a sudden change of tone, "you've been absent from town for exactly nine days, until yesterday morning. Just where have you spent those nine days?"

Harvey Grimm moved to the sideboard and helped himself to a cigarette from an open box.

"Well," he observed, "I'm hanged if I can see that that's anybody's business except my own."

"I will admit, sir," Brodie proceeded, "that there is, at the present moment, not the slightest necessity why you should answer that question—it is, in fact, a matter slightly removed from the immediate object of our visit this morning—and yet it is a question which I am going to press upon you, and which, should you feel so disposed, Mr. Grimm, you might possibly answer with great benefit to yourself. The long and short of it is this. Is it worth your while to put yourself right with the authorities and with me, or isn't it? I tell you, as man to man, I have a theory of my own about you and your disappearances."

"I should have thought," Harvey Grimm remarked, after a brief pause, "that Inspector Ditchwater, having made himself so free with my apartments, would have been in a position to have told you everything himself. However, come this way...."

He led them into the bedroom. A portmanteau, not wholly unpacked, was open upon the stand.

"My portmanteau," he pointed out, "which, as you have doubtless already ascertained from the hall-porter, came back with me the night before last. There's the label."

Mr. Brodie turned it over and examined it.

"Exford," he murmured.

"Just so," Harvey Grimm assented. "Now what about those two sets of fishing-rods there?"

The detective fingered the label and read the address aloud.

"Mr. Harvey Grimm,
The Crown Hotel, Exford."

"That, of course," Harvey Grimm continued drily, "is not evidence, as the label is in my own handwriting, but you will find that the golf clubs there bear a railway label, I think."

The detective turned the bag around and nodded.

"Very interesting," he admitted, "but Exford—at this time of the year!"

"You're no sportsman, Brodie," Harvey Grimm said reproachfully, "or you'd know all about the March trout. Just a moment. Come back into the sitting-room."

He led the way, searched for a moment on the sideboard and threw a *Daily Mirror* on to the table. Brodie adjusted his eyeglasses. In the left-hand corner of one of the inner pages was a small picture of a man fishing, and underneath:—

Fine catch of Mr. Harvey Grimm, a London
sportsman, in the River Exe, last Monday.

"Quite a good likeness, too," the detective observed, as he laid down the newspaper. "Say, this is very interesting, Grimm! It disposes altogether of one of my theories. I had no idea that you possessed such simple tastes. I've done a little sea-fishing myself. Well, well!"

"Still,"—now, Ditchwater!—"you got back in time last night to help yourself to Madame de Borria's necklace!"

It was all an affair of seconds. Ditchwater had suddenly caught Harvey Grimm's two arms from behind whilst Brodie's hand had dived into his coat pocket. The necklace glittered upon the table. There was a moment's intense silence. Brodie was breathing quickly. There was a gleam of triumph in his eyes.

"Dear me," Harvey Grimm exclaimed, "fancy your finding that!"

The detective bent over his prize.

"The middle diamond is, without doubt," he announced, "a rose diamond. Quite a peculiar red light. Ditchwater, step round to Madame de Borria's rooms. Ask her if she will be so good as to come here at once."

The inspector disappeared. Harvey Grimm relit his cigarette, took off his overcoat in a dazed way, threw it over the back of a chair, and hung up his hat.

"I shouldn't bother to do that. Grimm," the detective advised him quietly. "I am afraid we shall have to ask you to come and pay us a little visit. You've got plenty of common sense, I know. It isn't necessary, I suppose, to tell you that there are a couple more men in the corridor?"

"I've no idea of making a fool of myself," Harvey Grimm replied, "but do you mind if I help myself to a whisky and soda? Your methods are a little nerve-shaking."

The detective stepped in front of the sideboard.

"Say, I don't believe for a moment. Grimm," he said, "that you're up against it badly enough for that, but I don't think I'd worry about a drink just now."

"Mix it for me yourself, then," the other suggested.

The detective hesitated for a moment, and then did as he was asked, keeping his back, however, to the sideboard, and reaching first for the whisky and then for the soda-water.

"Say when?" he invited courteously, with his hand on the siphon.

"That'll do nicely. Thank you, Brodie. Your very good health!".

Harvey Grimm drained the tumbler and set it down. Almost as he did so, there was a knock at the door, the sound of voices and Madame de Borria entered. The detective had just time to throw a newspaper over the necklace before she appeared.

"You sent for me?" she exclaimed, turning at once to Brodie. "Tell me, have you news of my necklace?"

"Do you mind just running over its points once more?" Brodie asked.

She made a little grimace.

"I wrote it all out for Scotland Yard," she reminded him impatiently. "The stones are very fine but without any special character. There are sixty-three of them, almost equal in size until you come to the front. It is the front that is so wonderful. The middle stone is a rose diamond, the only one in the world which flashes a natural pink cross. There is nothing else like it. The two on either side are slightly pink, and there is one yellow one, two places from the middle stone. But it is the middle stone. Mr. Brodie, that is worth all the rest put together. It is the most wonderful in the world. Please do not keep me in suspense."

The detective lifted the newspaper from the table. It was seldom that he permitted himself any emotion. There was a slight gesture of triumph, however, as he turned towards the woman. She literally sprang upon the necklace, turned it over, gazed at it blankly for a moment and flung it back upon, the table.

"You brought me here to look at this!" she exclaimed contemptuously,— "and after you have heard my description too! Why, my necklace has twice as many stones, and my rose diamond has the flash of the cross!"

Both Brodie and the inspector stood for a moment as though stupefied, incapable of speech. Harvey Grimm threw his cigarette into the hearth.

"Madame de Borria," he said, "I should, perhaps, add my apologies to those which our good friend there is engaged in framing. The necklace is mine, or rather it is entrusted to me for sale. I am well aware that it does not resemble yours, which I have often seen and admired. Mr. Brodie, however, in his excessive zeal, gave me no time for explanations. He descended upon my rooms, seized the necklace from my overcoat pocket—scarcely a likely receptacle. I think, for stolen goods," he added, with a little expostulatory grimace—"and sent, off for you."

The lady turned almost savagely upon the detective.

"So this is the way," she said, "you conduct your affairs. Mr. Paul Brodie! You insult a harmless gentleman whom no one but an idiot could mistake for a thief, you drag me from my room to look at a necklace which does not resemble mine in the slightest, and meanwhile the thief gets further and further away," she added, with biting sarcasm. "Oh, you are very busy, are you not, catching him! You are very near that two thousand pounds!"

She stamped her foot and turned away. Brodie opened the door for her. His attitude was apologetic—almost cringing.

"Madame de Borria," he said. "I'm sorry. But two necklaces! Who could conceive such a thing! Rest assured, however, that this is not the end."

She strode away without another word. Brodie came back into the room. He fingered the brim of his hat thoughtfully.

"Say, are you in the habit of carrying valuable necklaces about with you in your overcoat pocket, Grimm?" he asked.

Harvey Grimm took up his stand very deliberately on the hearthrug.

"I am," he announced. "I also occasionally wear a coronet instead of a hat, and a suit of armour instead of pyjamas. I do these things because I choose, and because it's damned well no one else's business except my own."

"So you're going to take that tone, are you?" Brodie observed thoughtfully.

"Between ourselves, I think it's time I did," was the prompt reply. "The sooner you make up your mind that I am a harmless individual, the better. I told you openly, within twenty-four hours of making your acquaintance upon the steamer, that I was an expert in precious stones. That is how I make my living, and it is perhaps as reputable a way as yours. The necklace which you have had the impertinence to accuse me of stealing, is entrusted to me for sale, and if at any time, there was any real reason for me to disclose the name of the owner. I would do so. At present, however, I consider that I have humoured you far enough. You will oblige me by leaving my rooms at once and taking Inspector Ditchwater with you."

"So that's the line, eh?"

"That is the line," Harvey Grimm assented, "and what are you going to do about it?"

"Personally," Inspector Ditchwater decided, turning towards the door. "I am going to wish you good morning, and offer you my apologies, Mr. Grimm. We seem to be always in the wrong when we act upon Mr. Brodie's information, and the report I'm going to make to headquarters will perhaps save you any further trouble."

Brodie's face was imperturbable. He accepted the situation, however, and followed Ditchwater from the room. The two men left behind listened to their retreating footsteps. Harvey Grimm threw himself into an easy-chair.

"So that's that," he observed. "An exciting quarter of an hour, eh. Aaron?"

"I am bewildered," Aaron Rodd admitted. "I don't understand, even now. Wasn't it Madame de Borria's necklace, then?"

"That one wasn't!"

"You don't mean to say that you've got two necklaces?"

"Feel in the other pocket," Harvey Grimm directed him.

Aaron obeyed. From the right-hand pocket of the overcoat which was hanging over the chair, he drew out a second and more beautiful necklace. As he held it before him, the cross flashed out from the rose diamond in the centre.

"Good God!" he exclaimed. "You mean to say that it was here all the time?"

"Of course it was. I told you that I was in a tight corner. He never gave me a chance to hide it. I knew these rooms would be searched. Fortunately, he chose the left-hand pocket of my overcoat instead of the right."

"What are you going to do with it?" Aaron asked breathlessly.

Harvey Grimm glanced at the clock. It was a quarter to one.

"You shall see," he replied. "Just open the door, will you? I think I heard someone ring. Put the necklace away first—in that drawer will do."

Aaron did as he was told. A short, dark man, dressed with extreme care, pushed past him into the room. It was the husband of Madame de Borria.

"I have come," he announced. "How is the good Mr. Grimm, and what is the news this morning?"

"The news is," Harvey Grimm told him, "that the detective your wife employed has been up here, searching for the necklace."

"Marvellous!" the little man declared, rolling himself a cigarette nervously. "How sagacious! What foresight! But as to results, eh…?"

Harvey Grimm, with a little sigh of relief, thrust his hand into the drawer, produced the necklace and handed it to the South American. Mr. de Borria's face glowed with satisfaction.

"I have had a leetle trouble with Madame," he announced, "but it is past. She agreed at last eagerly to the advertisement. You have seen it?"

Harvey Grimm nodded.

"Two thousand pounds reward and no questions asked," he murmured.

Mr. de Borria drew from his pocket a battered and soiled cardboard box, into which he proceeded to stow the necklace.

"I make a package here, as you see," he pointed out. "I have received an anonymous note which makes a demand upon my honour that, if I accede to its terms, I destroy it. It is destroyed!"

"The letter—?" Harvey Grimm began.

Mr. de Borria tapped his forehead.

"In the air—in my brain," he exclaimed. "What does it matter? It is destroyed. I go to the place named, I produce the two thousand pounds—behold!—and the necklace is mine."

He laid a pocketbook upon the table and drew out a sheaf of notes, which he carefully counted into two heaps. One he pushed towards Harvey Grimm, the other he replaced in his pocket. Then he smiled. He had the engaging smile of a child.

"So!" he pronounced. "We are all happy and contented. Madame my wife will wear her necklace tonight and once more rejoice. I shall have that thousand pounds in my pocket which is so necessary for a man like myself in this, your great city of gallantry and happiness. And you, my dear Mr. Harvey Grimm, who played the burglar and assisted me in my little scheme, you, too, have a thousand pounds. So! Now that all is well, shall we visit the little lady down in the American Bar? Afterwards, I will take a taxi just to nowhere, and I will come back in another taxi from nowhere. I shall break into my wife's rooms, and she will hold out her arms to me, and she will have her necklace, and I have got my thousand pounds. *Enfin!* Let us descend."

Harvey Grimm took up his hat and Aaron Rodd followed suit.

"It seems to me," Aaron remarked, as he brought up the rear of the little procession, "that the only man who gets nothing out of this is Mr. Brodie!"

CHAPTER VII

THE INFIDELITY OF JACK LOVEJOY

Cresswell and Aaron Rodd were dining with Captain Brinnen and his sister at a corner table in the Milan Restaurant. Harvey Grimm had once more left them for an unknown destination, and they were all aware that the period of his absence would be this time more than ever one of strain. As though by general consent, however, the conversation did not touch upon personal matters. They spoke a good deal of the war. Brinnen himself was roused by sundry reflections into a momentary bitterness, an expression of that peculiar irritation common to many of his country-people, notwithstanding their underlying gratitude.

"You people in England," he declared, "you have no perceptions, no brains with which to combat a perfectly developed system of espionage; nothing but an infinite complacency, an infinite stupidity. The people who hate you walk in your midst, unharmed. Even if they are pointed out, your officials shrug their shoulders and smile in a superior fashion. 'They can do us no harm,' they assure you. 'There are reasons why we prefer to leave them alone.' And you are at war, you people! Ah, if only you would realise it!'

"You are quite right," Aaron Rodd admitted. "We have grown too accustomed to look upon espionage and secret service as the *bonne bouche* of the novelist. I suppose they do exist."

"They not only exist," Brinnen continued, "but they are becoming a very important factor in the progress of the war. Look at this room. Did you ever see a more cosmopolitan gathering! There are Belgians, Russians, Americans. The two young men who have just come in are Roumanians; over here no one knows why. This, however, I could tell you. If England takes no heed of their presence, Germany does. They will be watched by Germany until they leave, and, for all your army of censors, Germany will know, day by day, just what they do. And, even nearer to us, I could give your Secret Service a very useful piece of advice concerning the young man of the third table from here, with the lady in white spangles."

Aaron Rodd and the poet both glanced cautiously in the direction indicated. A tall, clean-shaven young man, dark, with big black eyes, a mass of sleekly brushed black hair and rather puffy cheeks, good-looking in a stagey sort of way, was entertaining an artistically decorated young ornament of the musical comedy stage.

"You know him, perhaps?" Brinnen inquired.

Both men shook their heads.

"He is always about here," Cresswell remarked; "generally in the bar."

"He is an American actor," Brinnen continued. "His name on the programmes is Jack Lovejoy. His real name is Karl Festenheim; he was born in Cologne. His father and his grandfather, his mother and his grandmother, were Germans. He married a German wife—a negligible affair, perhaps, as the matrimonial arrangements of those sort of people are inclined to be, but still it shows his tendencies. The man, like many thousands of others, calls himself an American because he went there as a boy and has lived there ever since. Yet every relative he has lives in Germany, every spark of real feeling such a person may happen to possess is German, he eats like a German, he lives like a German, he even talks like one. Yet that young man has no difficulty about passports. He can live in London, listen to the secret voices of your nation, and make his way unhindered and unharmed over to Germany whenever he chooses."

"There are, of course, many technical difficulties," Aaron Rodd pointed out, "in dealing with naturalised Americans, whatever the country of their birth."

"You are very punctilious over here," Captain Brinnen observed, with fine sarcasm. "However, I give that young man as an instance, because I know that certain information concerning the whereabouts of three of your cruisers, earlier in the war, was conveyed by him to the German Admiralty. I cannot prove this, but I know it. I also know that while, if you speak to him, he will tell you that he is out of a job, that the war has played the deuce with musical comedy, he refused three parts within the last month, on some pretext or another, because he is better occupied."

Stephen Cresswell sat up in his place. An expectant light shone in his eyes.

"An adventure!" he murmured.

"If you, sir," Brinnen remarked, "could develop the sagacity of a French or German Secret Service man, and fasten upon the life of that young man, you would probably gain the adventure which you seek."

"I am the very man for the task," the poet declared eagerly. "I have stuck like a leech to my friend Aaron Rodd here, in the hopes of travelling with him a little way into the land where adventures are as plentiful as gooseberries. The only one to which he has introduced me has been highly satisfactory, in its way," he declared, bowing to Henriette, "and the remembrance of it will be a happiness to me all my life, but one cannot live on one adventure alone. I am eager for more. I claim that young man, Rodd, do you hear? I claim him."

"He is yours," the other acquiesced grimly. "Poor fellow! One is almost inclined to pity him."

Cresswell smiled in superior fashion.

"My dear fellow," he said, "you are, without doubt, a man of energy and brains, but what you lack is initiative. Initiative is the gift vouchsafed to genius. I have genius, therefore I have initiative. To you, the affair connected with this young man appears at present to be as impenetrable as a blank wall. You would not know where to start. Wait. You shall watch my methods."

"In the meantime," Henriette whispered, gazing intently towards the doorway, "behold, Madame de Borria and her recovered necklace!"

They all turned their heads. The South American woman was on her way through the room, and around her neck flashed the light from her wonderful necklace. Aaron Rodd leaned a little forward in his chair.

"She is soon wearing it again," he remarked.

Brinnen shrugged his shoulders.

"Why not? It was lost only for a few hours. Madame had the good sense to follow her husband's advice and to offer that greatest of lures to the educated thief—a reward and no questions asked. Madame deserves to have recovered her necklace—and it becomes her well.... Shall we take our coffee outside?"

They all rose to their feet and left the restaurant together. The poet thrust his arm through Brinnen's and led him on one side, talking earnestly. Aaron was left alone for a few minutes with Henriette. They found a corner as far as possible from the strains of the over-persistent band.

"It is three months today," he reminded her, "since I saw you first in the gardens of the Embankment."

"What a memory!" she murmured. "And I, like the very forward person you have since discovered me to be, made tentative overtures to you with the object of discovering whether you were a lawyer not too squeamish about your clients or their business."

His face hardened a little.

"Are we coming soon," he asked, "to the end of your stock—or rather your brother's stock of jewels?"

"Why?" she whispered, looking up at him with slightly contracted eyebrows.

"Because I am tired of it," he declared frankly—"tired of it in connection with you, that is to say. I spend whole days, sometimes, in a positive state of terror. Luxury is a small thing compared with freedom and life. You have had over forty thousand pounds now. Why don't you take your grandfather somewhere away into the country? Even if you have to be content with half that sum, you could live on it and be safe. Let your brother go his own way. It isn't really worth while, Henriette."

She looked at the point of her slipper carefully for a moment. She wore a perfectly plain black velvet gown, and only a single pearl hanging from a strip of black velvet around her neck. Her fingers were ringless. Even her hair was arranged in the simplest of coils, yet there was no one else in the room quite like her.

"Henriette," he went on, leaning over her, "if you don't speak, I shall make a fool of myself."

She started, and looked timorously into his eyes. Then as quickly she looked away again. Her hands clasped the arms of her chair. She seemed suddenly interested in the orchestra.

"Say—what you were going to say," she begged.

"You know," he obeyed, almost roughly. "I am nearly forty years old. I have no money except the ten or fifteen thousand pounds I have made by helping to dispose of your stolen jewels, and I'm sick of it all—sick of it because I've found something in life worth living differently for. You know what that is. Leave your brother to live his own life. Bring your grandfather and come away somewhere, Henriette, and marry me. It sounds absurd, doesn't it," he went on, a little wistfully, "but in a way you've been so kind to me. You must have known."

She suddenly laid her hand upon his. It was a delightful little gesture.

"Please don't say any more just now," she implored. "I shall remember every word that you have said, and I don't think I have ever felt so much like—"

"Like what?"

"Doing what you ask," she continued quickly. "There! Just now—for a little time—we must think of other things. You see, here come my brother and Mr. Cresswell. Whatever is Mr. Cresswell going to do? Look!"

The American actor and his companion had taken seats almost opposite to them. Suddenly Cresswell left his host's side and crossed the room towards them. With a slight bow he addressed Lovejoy. Brinnen, who had strolled over to where his sister and Aaron Rodd were seated, smiled a little cynically.

"What you call, in your expressive language, rather the methods of a bull in a china shop," he observed. "I fancy that we shall see our friend return, a little chastened."

"You don't know Stephen," his friend murmured. "He has more confidence than any other man on earth. Look!"

A waiter had been summoned to bring a chair. The poet was seated now next the young lady, to whom he had just been introduced. They were all three chatting amiably. A waiter was receiving an order for coffee and liqueurs.

"That is what he calls initiative," Henriette whispered.

"The first steps are easy," Brinnen remarked, "and, after all, one must remember that Lovejoy is by no means a clever person. He is conceited and bumptious. Well, at any rate we must wish Mr. Cresswell luck."

"I was just asking your sister," Aaron said abruptly, "whether we were almost coming to the end of your hidden stores."

The young Belgian glanced around for a moment quickly and flicked the ash from his cigarette.

"Why?"

"Because I am beginning to fear the risk more every day for your sister's sake," Aaron continued steadily. "Our friend Mr. Brodie has made a good many mistakes, but he is not an entire fool. Grimm admitted only the other day that he had tracked him down to the very place where he re-cuts the diamonds—had been within a few feet of them."

"Nothing came of it, though," Brinnen observed, frowning.

"It may not be so every time," Aaron Rodd persisted. "I was trying to persuade your sister to be content with small things. Your grandfather is very old. Think what the shock would be to him if anything were to happen to either of you. Put what you have left in a safe deposit, if you like, for a time, and start again disposing of them when things have blown over a little."

The brother and sister exchanged glances which to Aaron Rodd were inexplicable.

"What does Mr. Harvey Grimm say about it?" the former asked.

"Oh! Grimm will go on till he drops," Aaron Rodd declared. "Adventure, danger, whatever the cost, is the spice of life to him. But he is just a man alone. It's a different thing when a girl like your sister is concerned. It is for her sake that I want to see the thing closed up."

Brinnen dropped his eyeglass and rubbed it for a moment with his handkerchief.

"You seem to take a great interest in my sister, Mr. Rodd," he said calmly.

"I have just asked her to marry me," Aaron Rodd replied bluntly.

Brinnen turned slowly around. He was suddenly like his grandfather. His eyebrows were a little uplifted. His expression was the expression of one who listens to some unthinkable thing.

"Absurd!" he muttered.

"It is nothing of the sort," Aaron Rodd answered simply. "If your sister has been guiltily concerned in your adventurous life, I, too, have turned myself into a receiver of stolen property. We are in the same boat, only I want to get her out of it. I have asked her to marry me and come over to America. We could start life again on what I have."

She leaned over suddenly and spoke to her brother in a low tone, and in a language which was strange to Aaron Rodd. His expression changed a little as he listened. Then the waiter appeared with their coffee and liqueurs. When they were served and he had left. Captain Brinnen reopened the subject.

"I gather that you yourself, Mr. Rodd," he observed, "have hankerings towards the humdrum life, the life of honesty and the virtues and that sort of thing."

"I have tried for many years to make an honest living," Aaron replied shortly. "The only time I ever crossed the line was long ago, when Harvey Grimm and I were in America. It wasn't anything very serious then. Our present transactions have been my only other essay. I come of an old-fashioned New England family; and however one may laugh at their principles and the narrowness of their outlook, I have those principles in my blood, and, frankly, I hate this life. If it's bad for me, it's worse for your sister. I want to take her away."

"I will consider what you have said, Mr. Rodd," Brinnen replied. "For the present we will, if you please, abandon the conversation."

A little glance of entreaty from Henriette closed Aaron's lips. They spoke of general things for a few moments. Then Captain Brinnen rose to his feet.

"I am afraid that I must take my sister away now, Mr. Rodd," he announced. "She has an engagement for this evening. But before we leave," he added, holding out his hand, "whatever I may feel concerning the proposals you have made, I should like once more to express my thanks for your great courage the other night. My sister and I owe you more than we can ever repay."

"Your sister," Aaron said, with a boldness which surprised him, "can repay me if she will."

She looked into his eyes, and they seemed to him larger and softer than he had ever seen them. There was a little quiver at her lips, too, even though her words were light ones.

"You are growing into a courtier, Mr. Rodd," she murmured. "Au revoir!"

They passed up the stairs and Aaron sank back in his chair. There was a certain satisfaction mingled even with his disappointment. At least he had spoken his mind. Then the little group on the other side of the way arose, and the poet, catching his eye, beckoned to him in friendly fashion.

"This," the poet declared, as Aaron approached, "is my friend Aaron Rodd. Aaron, allow me to present you to a lady whom you have often worshipped from a distance, Miss Pamela Keane."

Aaron, who had no idea who Miss Pamela Keane was, bent over her hand and cursed the poet under his breath. The latter, who was thoroughly enjoying himself, laid his hand upon Lovejoy's shoulder.

"And also to my friend Mr. Jack Lovejoy," he continued. "Lovejoy is the one man in London who makes me wish that I could write for the musical comedy stage. One has one's limitations, alas!"

There followed a few minutes' desultory conversation. Then Miss Pamela Keane picked up a wonderful collection of golden trifles and turned towards the exit.

"We shall meet again, Mr. Cresswell," she said, smiling upon him. "Do bring Mr. Rodd with you, if he cares to come. Au revoir!"

She turned away, followed by Lovejoy. The poet linked his arm through Aaron's and demanded another liqueur.

"You didn't really know the fellow, did you?" Aaron asked curiously.

"Not I," he replied. "But, as I have told you many times, I am a born adventurer. I am equal to any situation. Have I ever mentioned that I am also something of a snob?"

"I don't seem to remember the confession."

"Well. I am. I have an aunt who is the wife of a baronet. I make use of her occasionally. In the days of my more abject poverty I used to go there for a free meal when I had a black coat. She is by way of being a patroness of the arts; entertains all sorts of jumbled-up parties. In all probability Mr. Lovejoy has either been asked to one of them or wishes he had. Hence my self-introduction. 'Mr. Lovejoy,' I say in my best manner, 'I believe I had the pleasure of meeting you at my aunt's, Lady Sittingley's?' He hesitates, and I can see that I have him fixed. He hasn't the least intention of ever denying that he was there, although he doesn't know me from Adam. And there you are, you know. It's the natural spirit of the adventurer."

"What was that about going on there tonight?" Aaron inquired.

"We are both going, my boy," was the cheerful reply. "Miss Pamela Keane is entertaining a few friends to *chemin de fer* at her flat in Buckingham Gate. I have explained that I do not play, but we are going to look in for a glass of wine and a chat. As a matter of fact, I just want to cast my eye over Lovejoy's' friends, do you see?"

"There's no need for me to come," Aaron Rodd protested.

"There is every need," the poet insisted, watching the arrival of the liqueurs with satisfaction. "I like companionship. I like some one with whom to compare impressions after such a visit as this. You may notice something which has escaped me."

Aaron frowned a little wearily.

"Captain Brinnen was probably talking quite at random," he remarked. "Lovejoy doesn't seem to be the type of man who'd take a serious interest in anything except his own pleasures."

"Quite right," the other agreed shrewdly. "But he might reasonably take an interest in the means of procuring those pleasures. And as to our jewel-collecting friend talking at random, I don't believe it. A man with a face and a character like his doesn't chatter. We'll just spruce up here a bit and follow them right along."

The two men spent the next two hours in entirely different fashion. Stephen Cresswell made a host of new friends with marvellous facility, flirted with many pretty but unnamed ladies, ate *pâté de foie gras* sandwiches and drank champagne as though it were his first meal of the day. Aaron, on the other hand, found the customary stiffness of his manner only intensified by the Bohemianism of his fellow-guests. The women, with their laughing eyes, their frankly flirtatious speeches, their general air of good-fellowship and lack of reserve, seemed to him simply intolerable. Every time he thought of Henriette, he hated his surroundings and longed for the solitude which, notwithstanding his efforts, he was only partially able to achieve. To escape the new acquaintances whom the poet was continually bringing up to him, he even played for an hour. Afterwards, when the rooms became more crowded, he escaped into a corner and sat looking on. It was exactly the sort of gathering he had expected—a good many young ladies from the stage with their escorts, a strong element of the betting fraternity, a theatrical agent or two, and a sprinkling of those nameless people, always well-dressed, always mysterious, who seem to pass through life so easily without toiling or spinning. He was just deciding that, so far as the object of their visit was concerned, the evening had been wasted, when Pamela Keane came suddenly across the room and sat down by his side.

"I want to talk to you, Mr. Rodd," she said, throwing herself back in a chair and displaying an amazing amount of white silk stocking.

"You are very kind," he murmured.

"Mr. Cresswell tells me that you are a lawyer?"

"That is so," Aaron admitted, a little startled.

"Where are your offices?"

"17, Manchester Street, Adelphi," he replied. "Third floor."

"Can I come and see you at eleven o'clock tomorrow morning?"

"With pleasure!"

"Good! I'll be there. Not a word to Jack, mind. Come and have a glass of champagne."

He drank his glass of champagne and watched his companion drink three. Then she floated off to greet some newcomers and Aaron made his escape. The poet caught him up in the hall.

"The usual sort of crowd here," he remarked, as they left the house. "Pretty hot lot, some of those bookmakers and jockeys, but I didn't see a soul whom I'd ever suspect of getting off his own little run. What about you?"

"Come and see me at twelve o'clock tomorrow morning," was all the poet could get out of his companion that night.

* * * *

Miss Pamela Keane was marvellously punctual. In a blue serge costume straight from Paris, a hat which was a marvel of simplicity, a wonderful veil and a wave of perfume, she swept into Aaron Rodd's room the next morning as eleven o'clock was striking. He handed her the clients' chair, into which she sank, a little breathless.

"Say, this is some climb," she remarked. "Don't you have any elevators in your offices on this side?"

"Plenty," he assured her. "I have a very small practice and these are out-of-the-way premises."

She lifted her veil. Her face was thick with powder and her eyes seemed to him artificially brightened. There was some stuff which he didn't understand upon her lashes, and in contradistinction to these, to him, somewhat ghastly allurements, her expression was hard, her tone, as she spoke, almost rasping.

"See here, Mr. Rodd," she began. "I have come to talk to you about Jack Lovejoy. Know anything about me?"

"Nothing," he confessed.

"I don't suppose you've ever seen me on the stage, even?"

"Never!"

"So much the better. I didn't want to go to one of these know-everybody-and-everything theatrical lawyers, who call you 'my dear' and promise you the earth. Well, I married a millionaire over in the States, and I fixed things so that he couldn't get rid of me without it costing him something. I've got an income of five thousand pounds a year, Mr. Rodd, and though that ain't the earth, it's useful."

"Naturally," he assented.

"I've done more than I should like to tell you for Jack Lovejoy," she went on. "Of course, we live together, and we're as much married as the law allows. He'd got nothing but what he was earning, and that wasn't much, when I took him up. Now he's got his motorcar and everything he wants. I'm not a changeable woman. I'm older than he is, of course, but I'm barely forty, and all I wanted of Jack was that he should play the game. He's not doing it, Mr. Rodd."

The lawyer shrugged his shoulders ever so slightly. The question of Lovejoy's infidelities appeared to him profoundly uninteresting.

"I'll tell you how I know," she went on. "We had a little trouble a month ago, and I've waited for him to come to me for his cheque since, instead of handing it over. He hasn't been, and he's had all the money he wanted. He's getting it from somewhere. What I want to know is where?"

Aaron was a little more interested.

"Betting? Card playing?" he suggested.

She waved her hand scornfully.

"I know the firm with whom he does his betting, and he owes them a tidy sum already. And as to card playing, why, any of 'em would clean him out in no time. He hasn't the brains of a rabbit. It's a woman. He goes to see her every day at six o'clock. I've found that out for myself, and I've found out the direction he goes in. For the rest I have come to you."

"To me?" Aaron exclaimed, a little startled.

"Yes! It's part of your job, ain't it? Supposing it was a divorce I wanted, I should have to go to a lawyer, shouldn't I? I'm not imagining you hang about street corners yourself, but you've got to employ some one to have him watched, and you've got to begin this afternoon. I can give you a start all right from luncheon time. He'll bring me anywhere I say—Milan Grill-room, today, at two o'clock. We shall leave there, perhaps, at half-past three, and he'll drive me home. From that point he'll have to be watched. He may come in for an hour or he may not, but it's where he goes to afterwards that I want to know. Will you take this job on. Mr. Rodd?"

"With pleasure," he agreed. "It's a little out of my line, but I think I can arrange it."

"Then that's that," the lady remarked, rising. "I've got to be at my dress-maker's at half-past. Ring me up when you've anything to report."

Aaron Rodd bowed his client down the stairs, went back to his office, and threw the windows wide-open. Then he telephoned for the poet.

"I am going to do a disgraceful thing," he told him, upon his arrival. "I am going to betray a client's confidence."

"Would it well out easier with the help of a matutinal?" the poet suggested, with a glance at the clock. "My throat's as dry as a lime kiln this morning."

Aaron shook his head and told the story.

"Now get at it," he enjoined, as he bundled him out. "It's your job, not mine, and I have a letter to write."

* * * *

The poet, a few days later, paid an afternoon call. He rang the bell of a flat in Northumberland Court, inquired for Mrs. Abrahams, and after a moment's hesitation was shown into a small drawing-room in which half a dozen people were seated. The lady who was evidently the hostess, a large, Jewish-looking woman, rose from her place on the couch and regarded him with mingled distrust and curiosity. The poet, however, who had seen Jack Lovejoy in a corner of the room, was not in the least abashed.

"You haven't forgotten me, I hope, Mrs. Abrahams?" he said, bending gallantly over her hesitating hand. "I met you at my aunt's. Lady Sittingley's, and you were kind enough to say that I might come and see you sometime. I ventured to bring you the small offering I promised you—my poems, bound now, I am thankful to say, with a little more dignity than when we last met."

Mrs. Abrahams' face cleared slightly, but she remained somewhat disturbed.

"Of course! You are Mr! Cresswell, aren't you, the poet? I remember the curious stories there were about the beginning of your popularity. You have really brought me that book? How charming of you!"

"I have promised myself this pleasure for a long time," Cresswell assured her.

"Let me see," she went on, making room for him by her side. "When was it that I met you at your aunt's?"

"I have no memory, even for such inspiring events," he confessed ingenuously, "but I think it was about three months ago."

She sighed gently.

"This terrible war," she murmured, "makes it difficult to remember anything. You will have some tea, Mr. Cresswell? Let me introduce you to Professor David."

The poet bowed to his neighbour and glanced around the little circle, winding up with a nod to Lovejoy, who seemed hopelessly out of place. They were, for the most part, a very gloomy and serious little company.

"I interrupted an interesting conversation, I am sure," the poet declared genially. "May it not continue?".

There was a moment's rather awkward silence, and Mrs. Abrahams sighed.

"Alas!" she said, "I am afraid there was nothing original about our conversation this afternoon. It was the war—always the war."

Cresswell balanced his plate upon his knee, sipped his tea, and talked commonplace nonsense for a quarter of an hour. Then he got up to leave.

"Coming my way, Lovejoy?" he inquired.

The young actor hesitated for a moment and then acquiesced. Mrs. Abrahams bade them both farewell. She extended to neither of them any invitation to return.

"Rather a heavy sort of crowd for you, isn't it?" Cresswell asked, as they descended in the lift.

"Mrs. Abrahams was kind to me when I first came to London," Lovejoy remarked, a little vaguely. "I promised I'd look in there some day, and I happened to be near this afternoon."

"Just so," the poet murmured, as they paused at the corner of the street. "So long!"

Jack Lovejoy stepped into a taxi and was driven away westwards. Cresswell crossed the road, turned into Whitehall, made his way into a block of public buildings, and after half an hour's delay was shown into the presence of an important-looking gentleman, who bade him take a seat and peered at him doubtfully over the top of his eyeglasses.

"Sir Lionel," his visitor began, "I have come to you because I have some information which should be exceedingly valuable to the home branch of the Secret Service."

"Young man," the official replied, "you are the fifteenth caller within the last few hours who has brought me information guaranteed to save the Empire."

"Lucky number, the fifteenth," the poet remarked cheerfully. "Do you happen to know Mrs. Abrahams of Northumberland Court?"

"I know her slightly," Sir Lionel admitted. "She is a friend of several members of the Cabinet."

"Why isn't she interned?" Cresswell demanded. "She is a German."

"Her husband was born in England."

"But she is a red-hot German, all the same," the young man persisted. "I have been making inquiries about her myself, and I find that for years before the war she was doing nothing but run down the culture and customs of this country as compared with Germany."

The official shrugged his shoulders.

"There is no information that I am aware of against Mrs. Abrahams," he said, "and you must remember that she is, as I told you, a friend of several members of the Cabinet. They would not be likely to listen to anything against her."

"What a country!" the poet sighed. "What officialdom! What methods of making war!"

"Have you anything against Mrs. Abrahams?" Sir Lionel inquired.

"I have," was the prompt reply. "I have no proof to offer because I am an unofficial person and I cannot take those steps which are necessary to procure proof, but I can assure you that every afternoon, from four till six, Mrs. Abrahams' drawing-room in Northumberland Court is a bureau for the meeting of various persons whose interests are inimical to this country."

"Dear me!" the other exclaimed blandly. "What do they do there?"

"I can't tell that," Cresswell admitted. "My idea is that they each bring information of various sorts, which Mrs. Abrahams transmits to Germany."

"Isn't that rather an assumption on your part?"

"An assumption with a very definite background," the poet persisted unruffled. "For instance, take this afternoon. Amongst Mrs. Abrahams' visitors were Professor David, who has spent half his life in Germany, has stumped this country, lecturing on German ideals, and since the war has maintained a sedulous and enigmatic silence. There were also present Mr. Halstan, who married a German and has had to resign his seat in Parliament owing to his doubtful sympathies; Jack Lovejoy, the German-American actor; two men who, from their conversation, are, I gathered, censors; and the Minister of a country whom we all know quite well to be inimical to us. These men meet every afternoon. They aren't there for fun, are they? and it isn't by chance that they all have the same point of view."

Sir Lionel stifled what seemed suspiciously like a yawn.

"You must forgive me if I seem a little unmoved," he observed, "but we hear so many of these vague stories. The matter shall be looked into, Mr. Cresswell, but I may as well warn you at once that Mrs. Abrahams has several friends in the Cabinet, and they are not likely to countenance any proceedings unfavourable to her."

The poet rose from his chair.

"Thank you, Sir Lionel," he said humbly. "I begin to realise—"

"What?"

"That a friend of a Cabinet Minister in this Government can do no wrong," the young man declared, picking up his hat.

* * * *

Aaron Rodd and the poet lunched together the next day at the Milan. Miss Pamela Keane saw them from the other end of the room, where she was talking to the *maître d'hôtel* about a table, and at once came over towards them.

"Well?" she asked Aaron Rodd.

"I have some information already," the latter replied. "I am not in a position to make a definite report, but if it interests you to know it, I do not think that Mr. Lovejoy's afternoon philanderings are of an amorous nature."

"Say, do you hear that!" she exclaimed, her face suddenly lightening. "If it interests me to know it! Isn't that exactly what I came to you for? Well, can't you give me an idea what he is up to, then?"

"Not at present," Aaron Rodd regretted, "but you might, if you would, help me with another hint."

"Get on with it, then," the lady urged. "He may come in at any moment."

"Can you tell me in which direction his sympathies lie with regard to the war?"

Miss Pamela Keane was for a moment serious. Then she shrugged her shoulders.

"Well, you know," she said, "there are a good many of us Americans who think that Great Britain's been asking for trouble for some years back. A little too much of the Lord Almighty, you know. I shouldn't say that Jack was overmuch in sympathy with you Britishers."

"That helps," Aaron Rodd admitted. "In two or three days at the most I think I can let you have a report. So far as I can see at present," he added. "I think that it will be satisfactory to you."

"Say, you're smarter than you look, Mr. Rodd," she declared, as she turned away with a little nod. "Come round and see me any time."

The two men finished their luncheon and walked round to Scotland Yard. Inspector Ditchwater, for whom they inquired, received them with some surprise.

"Gentlemen," he said, "this is a most unexpected pleasure."

"We have come," Aaron Rodd began, "to lay certain information before you which has come to me professionally, and to ask for your aid. The facts are these. A certain Mrs. Abrahams, who is a German woman by birth, married to an anglicised German Jew, who was naturalised fifteen years ago, is in the habit of receiving a little circle of friends every afternoon. These friends are every one of them of more or less German sympathies, although some of them occupy public posts in this country. One of them, I have reason to know, is receiving money continually from Mrs. Abrahams. I have no proof of anything, and I am not in a position to proceed far enough in the matter to secure it. The authority of the law is needed. My friend here, Mr. Cresswell, has been to the Home Office and has interviewed Sir Lionel Rastall. He, however, declines to intervene in the matter because Mrs. Abrahams, who is a woman of a great deal of superficial culture and many acquaintances, is a friend of several Cabinet Ministers."

"If Sir Lionel declines to interfere," the inspector pointed out, "what can we do?"

"Get on to the track and find some proof," Aaron Rodd suggested. "There isn't any one can stop you then from behaving in a common-sense manner."

"And lose our promotion and get snubbed for our pains," the detective remarked. "I don't care much about the job, Mr. Rodd, thanking you all the same. I don't mind telling you that Mrs. Abrahams was on the list of suspected persons kept here, and has been crossed off at the special instructions of a highly placed personage. It isn't my business to interfere with her or her doings."

The two visitors withdrew, a little perplexed. The poet, however, was undaunted.

"My friend," he said, "this was to be my adventure, and I tell you I've a trump card left yet. Come along."

They paid one more call at a large and imposing establishment no great distance away. After a wait of nearly an hour an orderly came in.

"The Chief will see you and your friend, Mr. Cresswell," he announced. "Be as quick as you can, please."

The poet, who loved words, showed that he knew how to dispense with them. He shook hands with the somewhat grizzled-looking, handsome soldier who welcomed them.

"This is my friend Mr. Rodd, a solicitor," he said. "Sir Horace, I have put my hand by accident upon a nest of conspiracy within a quarter of a mile from here. The Home Office or the police won't touch it because the woman chiefly concerned is *persona grata* with Cabinet Ministers. Will you take it on?"

"I will," Sir Horace promised, "if there's anything in it. Get on with your information."

"The woman's name is Abrahams, and she has a flat in Northumberland Court," the poet continued. "I followed a young man there the other afternoon, who is a born German but calls himself an American. Mrs. Abrahams was entertaining a small party of friends every one of whom is of German sympathies, although two are employed as censors by His Majesty's Government. The young man I followed is drawing, money from her nearly every week, and spends most of his spare time motoring round London with one of the new naval air defence commanders."

"That all?"

"Pretty well," the poet admitted, "but there's espionage work going on there every afternoon."

"Sounds probable," the other agreed. "Now what do you want me to do? I can't raid the place without more information."

"Lend me two men, and I'll take the risk of something turning up," the poet begged.

Sir Horace scribbled a few lines on a piece of paper.

"Get out with you," he said. "My regards to your aunt. Show this to the orderly in Room C, and he'll give you a couple of plainclothes policemen."

The poet gripped Aaron Rodd's arm triumphantly as they stepped outside.

"A man!" he exclaimed. "A man at last!"

* * * *

It was two days before anything fresh happened. Then, about half-past five in the afternoon, Aaron Rodd and the poet, who had wandered round by the front of Northumberland Court to see that their watchers were in position, almost ran into the arms of a huge, roughly dressed man, with close-cropped brown beard, a man who looked ill at ease in his clothes and walked with a rolling gait.

"My God!" the poet muttered. "It's the Dutchman! Come on, Aaron."

They turned round and followed him at a short distance. He entered Northumberland Court. They followed him, a few minutes later, and Cresswell addressed the hall-porter, whom he knew slightly.

"My name's Cresswell," he said. "I'm on a Government job. Tell me what flat that man asked for who had just gone in?"

"Number sixty-seven, sir," the man replied—"Mrs. Abrahams'."

"Seen him here before?"

"He comes about once a week, sir; generally on a Sunday."

"I sha'n't move from here," Cresswell declared, turning to his companion. "I shall hold on to that chap myself, if he comes out before we can get the men together. Will you hurry, Aaron? There's one at the corner of Parliament Street."

"And the other's here," a quiet voice said behind. "It's all right, Mr. Cresswell. I've sent for Jimmy. I saw that man go in. Know who he is?"

"I do that," the poet assented.

"His ship's been searched twice," the inspector went on. "We had a Secret Service man on board the last time they crossed. Nothing was discovered, but he's under suspicion. When I saw him turn in here, I thought things might be coming our way."

"Inspector," Cresswell asked eagerly, "your powers will allow you to hold him, won't they?"

"I think I'll have to stretch them a bit, sir," the man replied. "We'll wait till he comes out. You'd better let the hall-porter get an extra constable. This Dutchman is a pretty difficult customer to tackle."

The hall-porter, who had been divided between curiosity and nervousness, departed with alacrity. The men spread themselves out a little. The poet and Aaron Rodd affected great interest in the lighting of cigarettes. A small boy in buttons eyed them with immense inquisitiveness. There was something up! He whispered the news to the lift-boy, who had strolled out for a breath of fresh air. A ripple of electrical interest thrilled the group. The hall-porter returned, an unwilling constable in the rear.

"What's this?" he inquired of the elder of the two plain-clothes men. "I can't leave my beat unless there's a charge."

The man showed him a badge. The constable saluted.

"Wait just outside," the former whispered.

The hall-porter suddenly thrust his head through the swing-doors.

"Party you're inquiring for, sir, has just come out of number two," he announced. "He's stepping into a taxi."

There was a rush for the door, which the poet led. The taxicab was disappearing round the corner as they reached the entrance of the next block of flats. The hall-porter, still dangling his whistle, watched their approach with amazement.

"What address—that taxi?" the inspector asked quickly.

"Monico's, Shaftesbury Avenue."

"Another taxi, quick!"

The man blew his whistle. A taxicab from the rank obeyed the summons.

"The fellow can't suspect anything if he's really gone to the Monico," the inspector observed.

They all crowded into the vehicle. In a few minutes they were at the café. The poet gave a little sigh of relief as he peered eagerly around. Somehow or other, he felt that this was his own special adventure, and that the onus of its success rested upon him. At a table a little way in the room the Dutchman was seated, with a huge tumbler of what seemed to be brandy and water in front of him. He was in the act of striking a match to light a cigar which was already in the corner of his mouth. Suddenly his eyes fell upon the poet. A vague sense of recognition, coupled with a premonition of danger, seemed to oppress him. His frame seemed to grow tenser. Even underneath his clothes one could fancy that his muscles were stiffening. He watched the four men approach, and those few of the neighbouring loungers—who chanced to be looking that way held their breaths. The atmosphere around seemed to have become electric. The inspector stood by the Dutchman's table. Although he was not in uniform, his official bearing was unmistakable. "I want you, my man," he said. "You must come with me to the police-station."

"Why?"

"I am acting under special orders," the inspector told him. "I can satisfy you as to my authority. The thing is, are you coming quietly?"

Apparently the Dutchman was not, for pandemonium ensued. The inspector was no lightweight and he was on guard, but his adversary's rush was irresistible. He went crashing over against an opposite table, and the Dutchman's left fist sent the second man prostrate. The inspector, however, was not yet done for, and Aaron Rodd and Cresswell suddenly sprang simultaneously into the fray. Men and women leapt from their tables. There were shrieks, a crash of breaking glass. The policeman who had been knocked down staggered to his knees and blew his whistle furiously. The Dutchman, kicking, shaking, even trying to bite the poet's fingers, which had somehow seized his throat, dragged his assailants yard by yard towards the door. The whole place was in an uproar.

Suddenly the swing-doors were pushed open. Two uniformed constables hurried in. Even then the Dutchman did not abandon the struggle. He wrenched himself almost free from the three men who had momentarily relaxed their hold, dealt the leading constable a terrific blow, which only just missed the side of his head and knocked his helmet into pulp. That, however, was the end. The other constable was a powerful fellow, and within thirty seconds the Dutchman was handcuffed. There was a crowd now upon the pavement. The Dutchman, his face covered with blood and his eyes glaring like the eyes of a wild animal, was bustled into a taxi. Aaron and the poet were left behind. They were neither of them much the worse for the struggle, but Aaron's collar was torn to pieces and the poet's coat had been ripped down one side. A waiter was hovering around them admiringly.

"Bring you something to drink, gentlemen?" he suggested.

They drank a brandy and soda each. Then the poet rose. He was conscious of various bruises, but he was very happy.

"Home and seclusion, I think, for a time, my friend," he said. "What a heavenly scrap!"

Late that evening, a very immaculately dressed young man of most superior appearance discovered the poet seated in an easy-chair in his club, awaiting the midnight rush of journalists and actors. The young man presented a card.

"You will find my name there, sir," he said. "And also the Service on behalf of which I pay you this visit."

Cresswell scrutinised the card and sat up in his chair.

"Have a drink?" he suggested.

His visitor begged to be excused.

"The Chief asked me to find you at the earliest possible moment," he announced, "first of all to express his thanks and the thanks of his department for your valuable services."

"Had that Dutchman got the goods on him?" the poet asked eagerly.

"He had indeed! He was carrying documents of high importance which were obviously destined for our enemies," the young man said. "Their contents are to a certain extent a secret, and I am to ask you to add to your services by allowing the matter to slip from your memory."

"What's going to become of Mrs. Abrahams?" Cresswell inquired.

"We received an indirect suggestion tonight from the Home Office," the young man replied, "that the lady in question should be cautioned. If it is any relief to you, let me assure you that my chief is not the sort of man to listen to such tosh. The lady will be interned, whatever her friends may attempt on her behalf. Two of the other people implicated, both in the censor's office, I regret to say, will be shot. You appear to have discovered a bureau which existed for the purpose of collecting and dispatching abroad every week various items of information likely to be of service to our enemies."

"What'll the Dutchman get?"

The young man hesitated.

"I have already somewhat exceeded my latitude," he said gravely. "May I ask you to consider what I have said in confidence, to forget this little adventure, and never again in this fife to worry about the Dutchman?"

"I won't," the poet promised, with a chuckle. "By the by, what about Jack Lovejoy?"

"There is a reference only to some promised information from a person whom we concluded to be that young man," was the reply. "He has been asked to leave the country within twenty-four hours."

The young man took his leave, and a few moments later Aaron Rodd appeared. He was wearing a pearl pin of wonderful quality, which the poet eyed curiously.

"A little farewell present," the former explained, as he settled down, "from Miss Pamela Keane."

CHAPTER VIII

THE YELLOW EYE

At a few minutes before the popular dining hour, Aaron Rodd, having selected a table, ordered, in consultation with the chief *maître d'hôtel,* a small dinner, and possessed himself of a theatre guide, sat in the reception lounge of the Carlton Grill-room, awaiting the arrival of Henriette. There was a mirror exactly opposite to him, and as he sipped his cocktail he caught a glimpse of his own face. He set down his glass, momentarily startled. Somehow it seemed to him like being brought face to face with the ghost of his youth. He rose to his feet and lounged over towards the mirror on the pretext of examining some illustrated papers. In the intervals of glancing at them, he looked furtively at his own reflection, trying to account for the change he saw there. At the poet's earnest solicitation he had visited a first-class tailor, had bought the right shape of collar, had learnt to tie his evening bow with the proper twist. A personally conducted visit to a fashionable hairdresser had followed, and his fine black hair, no longer ragged and unkempt, was brushed back from a face which seemed, even to its owner, to have changed in some marvellous way during the last few months. He was, without a doubt, younger. There was a new expression about his lips, from which the hardness seemed to have gone, and, curiously enough, he was conscious that notwithstanding all his anxieties, never more poignant than at this particular moment, life had taken a sudden and sympathetic turn with him. Since the coming of Harvey Grimm, he had at last been lifted up from that weary rut of depression and ill-being; but since the coming of Henriette, he had been transported bodily into the world where human beings live, where the flowers have a different perfume, and the sun shines always, even if sometimes from behind the clouds.

"But you, then, also are vain!" a rather surprised, very amused voice exclaimed almost in his ears. "Why, you remind me of Mr. Cresswell, standing there preening yourself before the mirror!"

For a moment he felt almost embarrassed. Then he smiled as he bent over Henriette's fingers.

"I was wondering," he confessed, "what could have brought so great a change into my life—and then you came."

Her eyes softened as she looked at him. Her lips parted. She studied him for a moment appraisingly.

"You are changed, you know," she decided. "You look younger. You seem, somehow, to have moved from one world into another. You were looking very melancholy that first day when we met in the Gardens. I do not think that adventures have disagreed with you."

"If one could only stop them now!" he exclaimed eagerly.

She laid her ringer upon her lip. The *maître d'hôtel* stood bowing before them.

"Madame will come this way?"

Henriette approved of the table, approved of the dinner, approved of her companion. As for Aaron Rodd, the shadows which sometimes terrified him seemed to have passed far away into the background. He was deaf and dumb to the voices and glances of their neighbours, attracted by his companion's unanalysable elegance, her aristocratic little face with its flawless complexion, her little air—foreign, perhaps, but all the more attractive—of quaint, individual distinction. She wore no ornaments except the pearls which hung from her neck. Her hair, to his untutored eyes, might have been arranged with her own fingers. Her gown, as always, was black, this time of chiffon, and it was not for him to know that its simplicity represented the last word in fashion. He simply found her adorable, and dinner was almost concluded before she uttered a little cry.

"Why, we have not yet decided what theatre to go to!"

He sent for a messenger.

"Do try," she begged, "and get some seats for the *Casino*. I want so much to see the revue."

The boy brought them a plan of the theatre, and Aaron secured a small box. Very reluctantly they left their table a short time later.

"I have loved my dinner so," she declared, as they sat together in the taxi. "I think that I am getting greedy; everything tasted so good."

"And I think that I, too, am greedy," her companion whispered, leaning towards her, "because I want so much—even the greatest thing in the world could have to offer."

She suddenly clutched his arm with her white fingers, drew it tightly to her.

"Hold my fingers, please," she begged. "Sit just like this. Don't let us spoil anything. Will you be content, please?"

He leaned a little towards her. Her eyes were half pleading with his, half doubtful.

"I will be content," he promised, "if ..."

She drew away from him a moment later.

"I did not mean to let you kiss me," she declared naively.

"I meant to if I could," he confessed.

She laughed a little hysterically, but not unhappily.

"Let us pretend that we have behaved like a couple of bad children," she said, "because we must not just now talk of these things. That was just a slip."

"A slip," he repeated.

"A very wonderful, delightful slip," she murmured. "And here we are."

They found themselves soon in a little box, small even for two people. Henriette settled down, almost from the first, to enjoy the performance. She laughed at the whimsical Frenchman, applauded the versatile leading lady, entered with wonderful facility into the spirit of the place. And then, some half-hour after their entrance, Aaron Rodd felt the fingers which he was holding under cover of a programme suddenly twitch. He glanced up. To his amazement, all the joy and light-heartedness had passed from her face. Her features seemed as though they might have been carved out of a piece of ivory. Her lips were a little parted, her eyes filled with fear. She was gazing with strange intensity upon the figure of a girl who, heralded by much applause, had suddenly bounded on to the stage. He leaned towards her.

"Is anything wrong, Henriette?" he asked softly.

She roused herself a little.

"Yes!" she whispered. "That, girl—do you see what she is wearing—around her neck?"

He glanced down on to the stage in puzzled fashion. The girl in question, French and a newcomer, who was singing a little song of the boulevards with a good deal of appropriate action, wore no jewellery except a single rather curious yellow stone, suspended from her neck by a platinum chain.

"You mean that yellow thing?"

She looked at him in surprise.

"But of course you do not know!" she exclaimed. "That is the great yellow diamond. It belongs to—"

"To whom?" he interrupted eagerly.

"To Leopold's—to my brother's collection," she explained hesitatingly.

He was puzzled for a moment. Then the sense of her words, and their import, began to dawn upon him.

"You mean that the stone is amongst those that your brother has acquired?" he continued diffidently—"one of those he has not yet tried to have re-cut?"

"Yes!" she murmured.

There was a moment's embarrassed silence. Henriette was obviously distraught. She watched the rather fascinating figure upon the stage with strained eyes.

"It isn't," she went on, turning abruptly to her companion, "that I mind if Leopold chooses to amuse himself. He has probably lent the girl the diamond for her first appearance. I see that it is her début tonight. It is not that. But he is so rash, so daring. That stone is known throughout the world—its history, its description have been published everywhere. Why, if there is anyone in the house who knows anything of the history of gems, they will recognise it. It will be traced—so easily traced to Leopold. Oh, what folly! I must go and see her. I must go at once!"

She rose to her feet. They drew a little into the background of the box.

"I am afraid it will be rather difficult," Aaron Rodd warned her.

"It must be arranged," she insisted. "We will go together and find some one at the box office who will take a message round."

They spent a more or less uncomfortable ten minutes at the box office, where they were assured that, owing to the smallness of the theatre, visits to the artistes were not permitted. The manager at last appeared and began an explanation on similar lines. Henriette interrupted him.

"Monsieur," she begged, "it is a great exception. There is something which Mademoiselle should know, something which it is very important for her to know, and I am the only person who can tell her. You will make an exception, please, this once?"

The manager was quite human and a person of discrimination. He made no further difficulty.

"If you will both please follow me," he invited. "Mademoiselle Larilly has just gone off."

He led them by a tortuous way to the back of the stage and knocked at the door of a room.

"*Entrez!*" was the shrill response.

Their guide ushered Henriette and Aaron Rodd into a tiny little apartment, prettily furnished notwithstanding the bare floors. Mademoiselle Larilly was standing before a pier-glass, admiring herself. She swept round at their entrance.

"Madame?" she murmured in surprise.

The manager spoke a hasty word or two of explanation, in French, and disappeared. Henriette waited until the door was closed. Then she turned to the girl.

"Mademoiselle," she said, "I owe you, perhaps, an apology for this unusual visit. I come for your sake as well as my own and another's. Will you tell me, please, who lent you the diamond which you wear?"

The girl held it tightly to her bosom.

"It has not been lent to me," she declared. "It is given."

"But that is not possible," Henriette protested. "Do you know that the jewel you are wearing is worth nearly a million francs?"

The girl started but she simply shrugged her shoulders.

"Oh, la, la!" she exclaimed. "What do I care? It was given me by a gentleman, not an Englishman, and no one has any right to ask me questions about it. I do not receive here, mademoiselle. I have but a few minutes to rest. If you would please go."

Henriette made efforts to modify the haughtiness of her tone, the air of aloofness with which she seemed shrouded.

"Mademoiselle Larilly," she said, "I will not believe that you wish evil things to the gentleman who lent or gave you that jewel, yet, believe me, you will bring harm upon him if you wear it in public. You will bring a great—the greatest of all misfortunes."

The girl opened her hands a little and gazed at the gem. She shook her head.

"That I cannot help," she decided. "It is his affair. He must know better than you. I promised him to wear it. He may even be here tonight. I shall keep my word."

"Mademoiselle—" Henriette began.

Then the words died away on her lips. The door of the dressing-room had opened and closed without any knock. Mr. Paul Brodie stood there, suave and with a little smile upon his lips. He bowed politely—a gesture which seemed to include everyone. Mademoiselle Larilly glanced at him contemptuously.

"But who allowed you to enter?" she demanded. "I do not receive here. I will send for the manager. It is an impertinence when people come to my room without permission."

Mr. Brodie held out his hand deprecatingly.

"Miss Larilly," he begged, "pray do not disturb yourself. I am one of those who must go anywhere they choose, at any time."

"Indeed!" she exclaimed indignantly. "You are not the owner of the theatre or the author of the revue, and I do not know you. I beg you to leave at once."

"Young lady," Mr. Brodie continued, his eyes fastened upon the gem which hung from her neck, "I have not the good fortune to be either of the gentlemen you mention, but I represent a force which has to be reckoned with by law-abiding people. I am of the police."

She stood quite still. Once more her hands clutched at the jewel which rested on her bosom.

"The police?" she repeated. "But I do not understand! What do you—what do the police want with me in my room?"

"Now come, Miss Larilly," Mr. Brodie went on soothingly, "it's nothing you need worry about. I just want your permission to examine the jewel which you are wearing."

"No!" she refused sharply. "No one shall do that. The jewel has been lent to me, lent to me on one condition—that I permit no one to touch it."

"Look here, young lady," Brodie protested, quietly but forcibly, "I don't want to make any disturbance, and I'd sooner deal with this matter in a friendly fashion. All the same, if you're out for trouble, I can soon bring you plenty of it. Come, it won't take you long to slip that off your neck."

She began to look a little frightened. She glanced towards Henriette as though for guidance. Henriette, however, seemed almost on the point of breaking down herself. She had sunk into the chair which Aaron had fetched.

"Courage," Aaron whispered in her ear. "That brute is watching you."

Brodie had drawn closer to Mademoiselle Larilly. She held her hands tightly against her bosom.

"If you come a step further," she cried, "I will shriek! I will call the artistes to defend me—the manager! You must come to me when I am not playing, if you would ask questions."

"Young lady," the detective said with a new sternness, "you can call the manager, if you will, and I shall repeat to him what I say to you. If you do not suffer me to examine that jewel, I shall stop the performance and have you taken to the police-station."

She was obviously terrified now. The rouge upon her checks seemed like a great daub of red. She set her teeth, her hands flew apart.

"It is a miserable country!" she exclaimed passionately. "In France this could not happen. Look, then, at the stone, and go, but remember—I will give it up to no one. If you take it, you must drag it from my neck and I will follow you, shrieking, even on to the stage. I will not be robbed! How do I know that you are of the police? You may be a thief yourself! The stone—I tell you that it is worth a fortune."

"I can well believe it," Brodie assented calmly. "One moment, if yon please."

He held the stone in the palm of his hand and fitted a magnifying glass into his eye. There was a moment's silence. Henriette suddenly gripped her companion's hand. Mademoiselle Larilly stood there, panting, her bosom rising and falling quickly. There was murder in her eyes. Presently Brodie let the stone fall, replaced the magnifying glass in his pocket. He stood, for a moment, as though thinking. Then he turned towards the door.

"Miss Larilly," he said, looking back at her, "my apologies. The bauble which you are wearing is a worthless piece of yellow crystal, worth, perhaps, twenty pounds. I was deceived—as was, perhaps, the young lady over yonder," he added with a little ironical bow—"by a wonderful resemblance."

He closed the door quietly behind him. There was a queer silence in the room. Henriette was deathly pale. Relief and bewilderment were struggling in her face. The French girl's expression had become electrically transformed. With a sudden little gesture she leaned towards the closed door. Her hand flashed in front of her face. Her gesture was significant if vulgar.

"It is worth twenty pounds, my bauble, is it?" she mocked. "And he thinks, that big, ugly man, that I would come on to the stage with a bauble round my neck worth twenty pounds! Eh, but he is not a gentleman of France, that—!"

An inner door suddenly opened. Leopold Brinnen appeared, and behind him the tall, slender figure of Monsieur Larkson, the leading French actor in the revue.

"With your permission," Brinnen began, bowing to Mademoiselle Larilly.... "Henriette!"

He stopped short in amazement. Henriette rose to her feet and came towards him.

"Leopold," she exclaimed, talking to him rapidly in French, "what have you done? How dare you, for all our sakes, run these awful risks! If the man Brodie had not been a fool, if he had known anything of jewels, if he had not been blind, where should we have been at this moment? Do you think they would have let mademoiselle go until she had told from whence came the Yellow Eye? Oh, but you are so reckless! Take it away from her quickly! Hide it!"

Leopold listened to her words a little gravely.

"Will you tell me, my sister," he enquired, "what you are doing here?"

"I have dined and am spending the evening with Mr. Aaron Rodd," she explained. "We sit in the box here and I recognise the Yellow Eye. I hurry here. Mademoiselle receives me. I beg her to take it off, not to wear it. I warn her that there is danger. She scoffs at me. And then Brodie comes. But that man—he must be mad! He held the stone in his hand."

The young man smiled quietly. Then he listened at the door which led into the passage and softly turned the key. He glanced towards mademoiselle.

"Ah, but if you all will," she exclaimed, "behold!"

Her hand disappeared for a moment down her back. She threw the platinum chain and stone which she was wearing, on to the dressing-table. In a moment another flashed upon her bosom.

"You see," she went on, "how simple! I obeyed. On the stage I wore that great beautiful stone, and even before I had reached my room, in the passage, the other hung in its place."

Leopold Brinnen smiled amiably. Nevertheless, he was a little apologetic as he turned towards his sister.

"It is that man Brodie," he sighed. "He is so persistent and yet he has not the wits for success. He wearies me with his blunders. This is just a little lesson."

"A little lesson," Henriette repeated reproachfully, with a sob in her throat, "which might have cost us—"

He waved his hand.

"Ah, no, little sister!" he protested. "You take too gloomy a view. Even Paul Brodie," he continued, lowering his voice so that it was inaudible at the other end of the room, "has not yet succeeded in forging the missing link between Jeremiah Sands and Captain Brinnen of the Belgian Artillery. You permit now, madame," he went on, turning back to the others, "that I present to you my sister and Monsieur Aaron Rodd. Mademoiselle Larilly," he explained, "is the wife of Monsieur Larkson here, whom I take the liberty also to present. What do you say? Which stone shall mademoiselle wear when she sings her next song?"

"One may play with fire a little too long," Aaron Rodd observed.

"Leopold!" his sister implored, clasping her hands.

The young man bowed.

"It shall be as you will," he promised, holding out his hand and accepting the stone which Mademoiselle Larilly was eagerly pressing upon him. "Into my pocket with this one, then. Madame shall dance for the first time in her life with a worthless bauble around her throat, but there shall be a recompense. I insist. We will all sup together at Ciro's. You agree? And you, Rodd? My sister," he added, "will, I am sure, be delighted to see more of you, madame, and your husband."

"It will give me the greatest pleasure," Henriette assented.

A call boy came shouting down the passage.

"Ciro's at eleven-thirty," Brinnen reminded them all.

"It shall be *au revoir*, then, madame!" Henriette said, as she passed through the door which Aaron was holding open for her.

* * * *

There was a great relief in Henriette's face as she leaned back in the darkest corner of the box and closed her eyes. The atmosphere of the evening, however, had departed. She was no longer full of that quivering, electrical gaiety. She watched the rest of the performance with interest and talked now and then to Aaron, but their homeward drive afterwards was performed almost in silence. She rested her fingers in his and leaned back.

"Forgive me if I rest," she murmured. "I am terrified. I shake now when I think of that moment."

"It is all over now," he reminded her. "Try and be quiet for a little time." Presently she sat up.

"Listen," she said, "it will be half an hour at least before they can arrive at Ciro's. Madame must change her toilette."

As Madame's last toilette had been one of pink silk, in which there was very much more stocking than skirt, the suggestion seemed probable.

"What would you like to do?" Aaron asked.

"I would like to call back at the Milan," she begged. "I nearly always see my grandfather for a moment before he goes to sleep, and I can rest and bathe my eyes. You will not mind waiting?"

"Of course not!"

He redirected the driver and they drew up, a few minutes later, at the Milan. She descended at the Court entrance and crossed over at once to the lift.

"I will not ask you up," she said. "I shall find you here, perhaps, in—say, ten minutes?"

He assented and bought an evening paper. In less than the time she had stated, the lift stopped and she reappeared. To his surprise she had taken off her hat. She came towards him with a strange look in her face. He could see the tears quivering in her eyes.

"Dear friend," she whispered, "be kind to me. I have had a great blow. My grandfather died this evening while we were away—only an hour ago."

He murmured an eager word or two of sympathy. She laid her hand upon his arm.

"Will you go, please, at once to Ciro's," she begged him, "and tell Leopold? Try and prevent him, if you can, entering the supper-room. There are so many things that will happen now," she went on. "Please go quickly. See!"

She raised her fingers to his lips. He caught them and kissed them. Then she turned away and he hurried outside, jumped into a taxi and drove to Ciro's. Leopold Brinnen and a little party of guests were standing in the hall. The former frowned as he entered alone.

"Where is my sister?" he demanded.

Aaron took him by the arm.

"Captain Brinnen," he said, "I am sorry, but I am the bearer of bad news. Your grandfather died this evening."

The young man stood perfectly still for a moment.

"Dead!" he muttered. "Poor fellow! ... dead!"

Inside the room the music was crashing, and the hum of conversation was already swelling to a tumult. A couple of early dancers were whirling round the room. Brinnen turned to his guests.

"I am so sorry," he explained, "Mr. Rodd here has brought me bad news. A near relative of mine has died suddenly. You must excuse my joining you. Luigi will serve the supper."

There was a little murmur of sympathy. His Bohemian friends crowded silently around him. One by one they shook his hand—a queer little function. Then he turned away and stood for a moment on the pavement outside, Aaron Rodd by his side.

"Mr. Rodd," he said, "my grandfather's death may make a difference in many ways."

Aaron Rodd straightened himself. He was never sure of the demeanour of this young adventurer, who seemed for the most part to treat life as a jest.

"In what way?" he asked.

Brinnen replied with a question.

"Can you communicate with Mr. Harvey Grimm?"

Aaron shook his head.

"I do not even know where he does his work. Forgive me for reminding you," he added, "that your sister is in great distress."

The young man stepped into a taxi.

"It is necessary that I see Harvey Grimm as soon as possible," he insisted.

"Harvey Grimm won't be hurried over his work," Aaron declared. "For your own sake he is better out of sight until it is concluded. Shall I tell the man to go to the Milan?"

Brinnen nodded. He leaned out of the window for a moment, however, before the cab started.

"Mr. Aaron Rodd," he said, "do you mind if I speak to you for a moment with perfect frankness?"

"Not in the least," Aaron assured him promptly.

"In some respects," Brinnen continued confidentially, "I am inclined to like you, but on the whole I have come to the conclusion that you are a very simple fellow. That is all!"

CHAPTER IX

THE VENGEANCE OF ROSA LETCHOWISKI

The small boy assumed an air of vast importance. He leaned over the counter and with mysterious gestures arrested the progress of his cousin through the shop.

"Rosa, I've got something to thay to you, motht important," he announced. "Come right over here."

She paused and swung around a little unwillingly. Her scarlet underlip was thrust outwards. She walked with her hand upon her hip, not averse to impressing even this young cousin of hers with all the allurements of her slipshod finery.

"I thay, Rosa, you look fine," the boy declared admiringly. "Lithen now. You told me to keep my eyes open, if ever I should see any more of Mr. Levy, eh?"

The girl's face was suddenly alight. She moved close to the counter.

"You've heard of him?" she exclaimed eagerly. "You know where he is?"

The boy nodded many times. He placed a finger upon his lips, in his eyes was the glint of avarice.

"You promithed me a shilling," he reminded her. "I worked hard. I know now just where he ith. You can see him for yourthelf. It's worth a shilling, Rosa, eh?"

The girl's hand dived into the recesses of her half-fastened skirt. She produced a cheap purse of imitation Russia leather and solemnly counted out a sixpence and six coppers.

"You tell me the truth," she adjured him, parting with the coins reluctantly.

"Honest and sure," the boy promised, sweeping them into his pocket. "He came back again Tuesday night. He's at work now in the repairing room."

"You little shark!" his cousin cried indignantly. "Why, I should have found out myself if I'd gone straight in to grandfather."

"Maybe and maybe not," he answered, with his finger upon his nose and his hand guarding the pocket where the shilling reposed.

The girl was breathing quickly with excitement. The loss of the shilling, after all, was a slight thing to a girl earning man's wages.

"Listen," she enjoined, "don't you say I've been. I'm off back to tidy up, I shall be here in half an hour. He won't be gone by then."

"Sure not," was the confident assent. "He brought his valise. He'th come to stop."

Rosa almost tiptoed her way out of the shop, dived into the stream of people and disappeared. It was rather more than half an hour before her small cousin, with palms outstretched upon the counter, struggling to sell a on-and-sixpenny brooch to a girl who had a shilling to spend, glanced up and recognised her. His look of admiration was a genuine tribute. For a moment the glamour of the transaction upon which he was engaged, faded.

"My, Rosa, you do look fine!" he exclaimed. "Them clothes must have cost something!"

She nodded haughtily—a vision of cheap furs, with a black hat from which flared one great scarlet flower. She carried a bag of some jingling metal in her hand. Her patent shoes squeaked loudly. She displayed at least twelve inches of silk-clad limbs, and she diffused little waves of a perfume carefully selected on account of its far-reaching qualities. The customer, who knew her by sight, gazed after her admiringly.

"That's your cousin Rosa, isn't it?" she asked.

The small boy nodded, withdrawing his eyes from the disappearing figure with reluctance.

"It must be wonderful to earn enough money to dress like that," he observed enviously. "My, did you see those furs! ... The firtht ornament Rosa ever bought from me wath one of these brooches," he went on, reverting to the subject in hand. "Two shillings she paid, my dear, and eighteenpence I'm asking you, jutht because I like to do business when the old man ain't here. Maybe you could pay the extra sixpence next Saturday...."

Rosa swept through the door and descended the two steps into the dingy sitting-room. In a high-backed chair drawn up to the scanty fire, his head a little on one side, sat her grandfather, asleep. She passed on tiptoe through the room, down the narrow passage, and softly turned the handle of the workshop door. The air was vibrating slightly with the monotonous hum of a concealed dynamo. Bending low over the board, with huge magnifying glasses in his eyes, Mr. Levy, with a small, bright instrument in his hand, was absorbed in some delicate process of refashioning a little glittering mass, carefully held between the thumb and forefinger of his left hand. Some instinct told the girl to keep silence. She watched him breathlessly until the consciousness of her presence reached him through his finer senses. He raised his knife from its task and turned swiftly around, touched a knob with his foot and the dynamo gradually slackened speed and died away.

"You!" he exclaimed, removing the glasses from his eyes.

She saw the stone upon which he had been working transferred swiftly to his pocket. She was immensely curious. Nevertheless, the personal element came first.

"You're a nice man, aren't you, eh?" she demanded, coming slowly towards him. "What about that little dinner we were going to have, eh, and a theatre? You just leave your place without a word of warning. I wonder grandfather took you back again."

"My dear young lady," he began.

"Rosa!" she pouted.

"Rosa, then," he went on, "pleasure is a great thing, but business is a greater. I have been away on business, the business I spoke to you of. Now, you see, I am back again. The other place didn't suit me."

"And grandfather took you on without a word?"

"As you see."

"What is it you are working at?" she asked curiously. "I never knew you had a dynamo here, or that you needed one for watch repairing."

"It is an idea of my own," he told her. "You see, it isn't only watches but every article of jewellery we repair. It saves another assistant."

"What were you working at when I came in?" she persisted.

"A piece of glass, cutting it up into a few of those beautiful diamond brooches you see in the window," he explained. "But don't let's talk, about the work. How well you look!"

She tossed her head.

"A lot you care about how well I look," she retorted, "going away like that with never a word!"

"By the by," he enquired suddenly, "how did you come in? Where was your grandfather?"

"Grandfather was asleep in the easy chair," she told him. "I came through on tiptoe. Like to keep yourself private down here, don't you?"

"Part of my training," he replied. "I can't work unless I am absolutely alone and undisturbed."

She leaned against his bench and raised her foot as though to look at the patent tip of her shoe. He was privileged to behold a goodly number of inches of silk-clad limb.

"What are you doing tonight," she asked, "after work?"

He shook his head disconsolately.

"Your grandfather is a hard taskmaster," he grumbled. "I generally stick on here until I'm tired out."

"We'll see about that," she promised. "Would you like … Oh, bother!" she broke off. "I promised to go to the pictures with Stolly Wykes."

Her companion's faint sigh of regret was very cleverly assumed.

"Perhaps another evening, then," he suggested.

"You're such a slippery customer," she went on, "here today-and-gone tomorrow sort of chap. I suppose I could put Stolly off," she went on meditatively, raising her eyes and looking at him.

"I wouldn't do that," he protested. "I can't help thinking how disappointed I should be in his place."

"Plenty of feeling for others you have, haven't you?" she observed sarcastically. "I don't know as I care about going out with Stolly. He's always worrying me to get engaged."

"I've wondered more than once," he told her confidentially, "why you haven't been engaged long ago. How old are you? Twenty?"

"I am twenty-two," she confessed, "and if I'm not engaged, it's because I haven't been over-anxious. I don't think much of these young fellows round here. I feel, somehow, as though I wanted something different."

He sighed sympathetically, and then, as though with an effort, turned back to his bench.

"If the old man wakes up and finds I'm not working," he remarked, "he'll be annoyed."

"You can get on with your work, then," she replied. "I'm going to talk to him for a minute or two. Be good."

She gave him a little backward nod, enigmatically encouraging, and left him, closing the door softly behind her. She made her way into the stuffy little parlour and shook her grandfather by the shoulder.

"Wake up, old man," she exhorted. "Nice thing going to sleep over the fire in the middle of the afternoon!"

"Eh, what—what, my dear?" he exclaimed, sitting up. "It's Rosa, is it? Ah! How beautiful you look, Rosa! But those furs—were they very expensive, my dear?"

"They were rather," the girl admitted complacently, "but I'm earning good money and want to get married."

"To get married, my dear," the old man repeated, a little vaguely. "Well, well, you find some young man with good prospects, and money—money in his hand, mind—"

"I've found the young man I'd like to marry," Rosa interrupted. "He's your assistant down there."

Abraham Letchowiski stretched out his hands in protest. He shook his head vigorously.

"No, no, my tear!" he cried. "You cannot marry him. He is just a journeyman repairer. He has no money saved. He spends too much on his clothes."

"He's a clever workman, isn't he?"

"Oh, he is clever," the old man admitted, "very clever indeed, but there are many clever people in the world who have not much money."

"Look here," the girl expostulated, "you're going to leave David and me your money, aren't you? You've no one else?"

"But I have not much," the old man whined, "and I may live quite some time yet."

"You're getting too old to work," the girl declared. "Why not take him into partnership?"

"Bartnership?" the old man shrieked. "Ah, my tear, you do not understand!"

"I understand the way to deal with you, anyhow," Rosa retorted. "You wait!"

She walked to the end of the passage and raised her voice.

"Mr. Levy, please to come here."

There was a smothered reply, and after a few moments he appeared.

Abraham Letchowiski, now thoroughly awake, sat in the chair, wringing his hands.

"Rosa," he exclaimed, "I implore you! Rosa! Listen to me!"

She cut him short. She seemed, somehow, to dominate the little room—strong, forceful and determined.

"Mr. Levy," she announced, "grandfather has something to say to you. He makes such a muddle of things that, although it is rather embarrassing, I shall say it myself. David and I are his heirs. He has saved a great deal of money."

"No, no, my tear—no!" the old man interrupted tearfully.

"He has saved a great deal of money," she went on placidly. "He has no other relatives. He is always bothering me to get married. I tell him today that I have made up my mind. If you are willing, Mr. Levy, he will take you into partnership. We will see that little David is done fairly with. Later on, when you grow older, he shall be your partner. Now, grandfather, sit up and hear what Mr. Levy has to say."

For once in his life, Harvey Grimm was taken at a disadvantage. He stood speechless and hopelessly astounded. Rosa held out her hands to him. Before he knew exactly where he was, he was holding one of them.

"So that's all settled," the girl pronounced, drawing him closer to her. "Now, grandfather, Mr. Levy—Edward we must call him now—is going to leave off work at once. We are going out to supper and a cinema."

The old man suddenly struck the table with his clenched fist. There was a curious solemnity in his voice.

"I will not have it!" he cried, his eyes flashing. "All that you have spoken is foolish, Rosa. I will not have this young man for my partner, nor shall you have him for your husband, even if he were willing."

"Why not?" she demanded.

"Because he is not of our faith," Abraham Letchowiski declared solemnly, "because his name is not Levy. He is not one of us."

Rosa was taken aback. She looked at her prospective suitor incredulously.

"Is that true?" she asked him. "I don't care twopence whether you're a Jew or not, but isn't your name Levy?"

"It is not," he confessed.

"Why don't you go about under your own name?"

There was a moment's silence. A sudden understanding leapt into the girl's face.

"Wait," she cried—"the dynamo downstairs, and those men who came here to search! What is it you do in that back room, eh?"

There was still silence. She passed her arms suddenly through his.

"Be sensible," she urged. "I am not a fool. I know that grandfather loves money and loves making it. So do I. If he lets you work secretly in his back room, it must he because you make money there. Well, why not? You need have no fear of me. Tell me the truth! I shall be faithful. I do not mind that you are not a Jew. I will marry you all the same. I like you better than any of the Jews I know."

Harvey Grimm wiped the perspiration from his forehead. It was a situation, this, for which no foresight could have provided.

"And I," Abraham Letchowiski thundered, "swear before the God of my fathers that you shall marry none but a Jew!"

The girl made a face at him and dragged him back into his easy chair.

"Don't you be a silly old man," she enjoined. "Times have changed since you were young. A girl has to have a husband, doesn't she? You wouldn't have me marry any of those skimpers that come around here?"

A fit of coughing seized the old man and he was momentarily speechless. She turned away from him.

"That's all right," she declared confidently. "He'll be reasonable by morning. You go and wash and get ready."

Harvey Grimm sighed mournfully. His wits were serving him at last, presenting a tardy possibility of escape.

"Miss Rosa," he said, "I haven't had the chance to say anything. You took me by surprise this afternoon. Perhaps I ought to have told you when we first met, but I didn't. I am married."

She stood looking at him for a moment, her voluptuous red lips parted, her eyebrows contracting.

"Married?" she exclaimed, a little hysterically. "You beast!"

"I can't help it," he apologised humbly. "I ought to have told you but I never thought. That is why I kept away before."

"I see," she murmured, with the air of one whose thoughts are far away.

Abraham Letchowiski sat up in his chair, he mopped his eyes with a yellow handkerchief.

"You see, my tear," he pointed out feverishly, "the young man is honest—he tells the truth. That is the end."

"Is it!" the girl muttered. "Perhaps! Anyway, he is going to take me out this evening. Your wife ain't here with you, is she?"

"No," he replied, "she is in America."

"Go and get yourself ready, then."

Harvey Grimm meekly acquiesced, and devoted himself for the rest of the evening towards the entertainment of his companion. The girl's manner was a little queer. At the restaurant to which he took her—the best in the neighbourhood—she appeared to thoroughly enjoy the lavish meal which he provided. She even held his hand under the table and smiled many times into his eyes. She took his arm as they walked through the streets, but in the theatre, which she chose in preference to a cinema, she sat most of the time silent and absorbed. On the way home she clung to his arm. When they reached the little jeweller's shop, she paused.

"Let me take you across to your rooms first," he suggested.

She shook her head.

"I want to find my handkerchief," she told him. "I must have left it in the parlour. Open the door, please."

He obeyed her, and they stumbled through the darkened shop, down the steps, into the close, stuffy little apartment. The remains of the fire were smouldering upon the hearth, but the room was unlit. Abraham Letchowiski and the boy had long since gone to bed. Suddenly she threw her arms around him.

"Kiss me!" she cried, in a choked tone.

He yielded, struggling, however, against her vehement embrace. His hands gripped her shoulders. He wrenched himself free. He stood on the other side of the table, for a moment, panting. Her eyes, luminous, shone through the darkness at him. Then suddenly she swung round, climbed the two steps, passed through the shop and closed the door softly. Almost immediately she reopened it. In the dim street light outside he could see the outline of her figure.

"Thank you very much, Mr. Married Man," she said, "for my evening."

He made no reply. There was a second's hesitation, a last opportunity, of which he declined to avail himself—then the door was closed. A few minutes later he locked it, went back to his workshop, and from a cupboard drew out a whisky bottle and some soda.

"Here's a cursed mess!" he muttered dolefully, as he mixed himself a drink.

* * * *

Mr. Paul Brodie laid down his cigar and newspaper and swung round in his chair to receive a visitor, already, in his mind, a prospective new client. A small boy had opened the door.

"The lady, sir," he announced.

Mr. Brodie recognised his visitor with a thrill of expectancy.

"Say, this is Miss Letchowiski, isn't it?" he exclaimed, holding out his hand. "Glad to see you, young lady. Please take a seat."

Rosa ignored the invitation. She came up to his desk and leaned over it.

"Look here," she said, "you're the man, aren't you, who came messing round my grandfather's jewellery shop a few weeks ago? You were after the assistant—Edward Levy."

"Well?" Brodie ejaculated eagerly.

"You bungled things, or else he was too clever for you," Rosa continued. "I've come to tell you that he's back again there now, carrying on the same game, got an electrical dynamo in the workshop, and no end of tools. His name ain't Levy at all, and he isn't a Jew."

"What do you suppose he is doing there?" Brodie enquired.

"Look here," the girl went on, "if I tell you, will you swear that you won't get my grandfather into this?"

"I think I can promise that," was the cautious reply.

"Breaking up diamonds, then—that's what he's doing," the girl confided. "He's at it now."

Mr. Brodie showed no signs of excitement, but he was already struggling into his overcoat.

"There will probably be a reward for this," he said to Rosa. "I shall not forget."

"I don't want your reward," the girl replied. "I've done it just because— well, never mind. You go and nab him."

* * * *

Brodie did not suffer the grass to grow beneath his feet. He drove straight to Scotland Yard, and chafed very much at the delay which kept him five minutes from Inspector Ditchwater's presence.

"Inspector," he announced, as soon as he was ushered into the latter's room, "I want you to give me a man and a warrant at once. This time I think I've got a clue that will lead us straight to Jerry Sands."

"Is that so?" the inspector remarked dryly. "We've been there before, you know."

"See here, Ditchwater," Brodie continued, "you've kind of lost faith in me, and I can't say that I'm altogether surprised. But just listen. The girl from Abraham Letchowiski's shop has been up to me today. She says that that fellow I went after is back again there. He's got a dynamo in the back place and a whole set of tools, and is breaking up diamonds. Just what I suspected before, only I couldn't lay my hands on him. This time we shall do it."

The inspector scribbled a few lines on a piece of paper.

"You can take your man," he said, "but don't get me into any trouble over this. We can't be raiding people's premises for ever, on suspicion."

"There'll be no trouble this time," Mr. Brodie promised triumphantly. "A jealous woman's the real thing in our job."

"Well, I wish you luck," the inspector replied. "If you're really on to Jerry Sands, you're on to a big thing."

Mr. Brodie, with a plain-clothes constable, took a taxicab to the Mile End Road. The two men entered the shop together. David was alone behind the counter.

"What can I show the shentlemen?" he enquired urbanely.

"We want to speak to your grandfather," Brodie announced. "You needn't leave the shop. I know the way."

They passed down the little steps into the stuffy parlour. Abraham Letchowiski was sitting in his chair, gazing into the fire and mumbling to himself. He looked at the visitors uneasily.

"What do you want here?" he asked. "I am not well today. I am not speaking of business."

"That's all right, Mr. Letchowiski," Brodie answered. "It's just a word with your assistant we're after."

The uneasiness in the old man's face changed into terror.

"What do you want with him?" he exclaimed. "He is a respectable young man, a very clever watchmaker. He comes from Switzerland. He has done nothing wrong."

Brodie turned to the constable.

"Don't let him move," he directed. "I can hear the dynamo stopping."

He ran down the passage and threw open the door. The man who had been working at the bench turned to face him. The whir of the dynamo was slackening, but Harvey Grimm had had no time to collect his tools. There were several curiously shaped knives and fine files and chisels lying about. Brodie saw them, and his eyes sparkled.

"Edward Levy," he said, "I arrest you on the charge of breaking up stolen diamonds. I have a constable in the room outside. You'll have to come up to the police-station with us and be questioned."

The young man laughed scornfully. He pointed to something bright held in the teeth of a small brass vice. With a touch of a finger he released it.

"Diamonds!" he scoffed. "Why, I am an expert on sham jewellery!"

Brodie pressed incautiously forward, and Harvey Grimm's left hand swung round with a lightning-like stroke. The detective went over like a log, groaned for a moment and staggered to his feet. Harvey Grimm pressed him back, forced his knotted handkerchief into his mouth, and closed and locked the door through which he had entered. Then he threw off his overall and caught up his coat and overcoat.

"You're a clever fellow, Paul Brodie," said to the writhing figure upon the floor. "Sorry I can't stop to discuss this matter with you."

He threw a little higher open the window which led into the yard, vaulted through and walked swiftly down the entry. He strolled into the broad thoroughfare, wiping the moisture from his forehead and looking everywhere for a taxi.

"My God!" he muttered to himself. "We coming near the end of things!"

Listening all the while for footsteps behind, which never came, he at last hailed a taxicab and was driven to Aldgate. At the Mansion House he alighted, and in another taxicab made his way to one of the streets on the north side of the Strand. Here he entered a passageway, climbed the stairs past a secondhand clothes shop, and on the second flight opened the door of a room with a latchkey which hung from his chain. He gave a little murmur of relief as he discovered a young man in a dressing-gown, seated in an armchair with his feet up on the mantelpiece, reading a paperbacked novel. The young man bore a remarkable resemblance to Mr. Harvey Grimm.

"Thank heaven you are in!" the newcomer exclaimed, commencing like lightning to throw off his clothes. "Turn on the bath, Jim—quick as you can—and take these clothes down to the shop. Shove 'em away anywhere."

The young man was already busying himself about the place.

"Anything wrong, sir?" he asked.

"I've just had the devil of a squeak," Harvey Grimm declared. "It'll be touch and go this time. How did I spend the morning?"

"We made a point of calling at your tailor, sir," the young man replied, "also your hosier. We looked in at Bendlebury's in Cork Street, and we had a cocktail—two, I think—at Fitz's bar."

"Capital!" Harvey Grimm muttered. "What did I do last night?"

"Last night we wore dinner clothes, sir," thee young man went on. "We dined at Romano's—"

"Alone, I trust?" Harvey Grimm snapped.

"Quite alone, sir," the young man assented. "We conversed for a time with two ladies at an adjoining table. Luigi spoke to us twice."

Harvey Grimm bolted through the door, and a few moments afterwards there was a sound of splashing. When he reappeared, a short time later, his complexion seemed to have undergone a marvellous change, and the most wonderful wig in the world had disappeared. The young man helped him into a blue serge suit. In five minutes he was dressed.

"My George, this is quick work!" Harvey Grimm murmured, his eyes sparkling. "There's ten pounds on the table, Jim. Put it in your pocket. I'll drop in tomorrow or the next day. Clean gloves and my malacca cane. Don't wait two moments after I've gone. Get rid of all the clothes I have been wearing, in the darkest corner of the store. There goes the wig," he added, throwing it on the fire. "There won't be any more Mile End for a little time. Get to work like blazes, Jim, and good-bye!"

The young man handed him a sheet of paper.

"There are our movements, sir, since you left last Wednesday. You will find about a dozen recognitions a day."

Harvey Grimm thrust the paper into his pocket, stole swiftly down the stairs, paused for a moment on the threshold—it was his one moment of danger—and then strolled jauntily out. The street was almost empty. A few seconds and he was in the Strand. He plunged into a tobacconist's shop, bought half-a-dozen cigarettes, one of which he lit, and a few minutes later he climbed the stairs leading to Aaron Rodd's office. There was no immediate answer to his knock, so he opened the door and stepped inside. A tall figure in khaki was standing in front of the looking-glass, going through sundry mysterious evolutions. Harvey Grimm stared at him in blank amazement.

"Good heavens!" he gasped. "It's Cresswell!"

The poet turned round and saluted Harvey Grimm in jaunty fashion.

"Cheero, Harvey!" he exclaimed. "You see, I've taken the plunge."

"Fine fellow," Harvey Grimm murmured. "Tell us about it?"

"I came in to tell Aaron," the poet went on, "but he is, for some unaccountable reason, absent. The fact is, at first I didn't feel the call of this sort of thing at all. In my soul I hate war today, that is in its external and material aspects—the ugliness, the bloodshed, the mangled bodies and all the rest of it. But a few days ago old Harris asked me to write them a patriotic poem. I tell you I no sooner got into the swim of it than I felt the fever burning in my own veins. I will read you the poem shortly. It will create a great sensation. The first person whom it brought into khaki was myself."

"You seem to have done the job pretty quickly," Harvey Grimm observed.

"I joined an Officers' Training Corps only a few days ago," Cresswell explained. "I went to my tailor's for a uniform and found that he had one made for a man exactly my height, who was down with pneumonia. So I just stepped into it and here I am. I came round to tell Aaron, to take a fond farewell and all that sort of thing. I'm afraid my adventures will be of a different sort for a time. We've had some fun, though," he added, with a reminiscent gleam in his eyes.

"We shall miss you," Harvey Grimm sighed, "but I am beginning to fancy that our own number's about up. I've had the narrowest shave of my life this morning, and I don't feel that I am out of the wood yet. Where is Aaron, I wonder?"

"He was out when I arrived," the poet replied. "I've been waiting here for an hour."

Harvey Grimm consulted his watch.

"It is time," he decided, "for number one. It is several days since I tasted a cocktail. After that we might lunch together."

The poet assented with alacrity. They left a note for Aaron and made their way round to the Milan. The bar was rather more crowded than usual and they took their cocktails to a settee in a corner of the room. Harvey Grimm sent for a page and wrote the name of Captain Brinnen on a piece of paper.

"Will you see whether you can find this gentleman in the hotel?" he directed. "He is staying, I believe, in the Court."

The boy departed. Harvey Grimm, who as a rule was a temperate man, drank up his cocktail quickly and sent for another.

"Do you believe in forebodings, Stephen?" he asked.

"I was brought up on them," the poet replied. "There is Irish blood in my veins. I am most superstitious."

"I have had an exciting adventure this morning," Harvey Grimm went on. "So far as any human being can see, I am out of it as I have been before. I have made the most careful arrangements, too—but there, it's well for you not to know too much. There's just this about it. I wish to God I could see that Belgian and get rid of a few baubles."

"Let me have them," his companion begged. "No one would suspect me."

Harvey Grimm shook his head.

"They're not your trouble, my hoy," he said. "Besides, you're too damned careless."

The page returned a few moments later.

"The gentleman left the hotel yesterday, sir," he announced. "The hall porter—"

"Well?" Harvey Grimm interrupted.

"The hall porter," the boy continued, a little confused, "said something about the gentleman having changed his name."

Harvey Grimm's face grew sterner, and the look of trouble about his eyes more pronounced. He put a shilling in the boy's hand and sent him away.

"There's something up here," he muttered. "First of all Aaron disappears, and now Brinnen has changed his name. My God, if they only knew what his other name really was!"

The poet chuckled.

"And to think," he murmured, "that I have been in it! What a man!"

"The devil of it is for me," Harvey Grimm declared, "that I've fifty thousand pounds' worth of his stolen jewels around my body at the present moment. I fought my way out of a trap this morning. I tell you, Stephen, as a rule this sort of thing stimulates me. I hold my head a little higher, I whistle gayer tunes, I am looking out for the bright things in life every second of the time, and my feet scarcely touch the earth. But today it's all different. I can't walk without turning round. I can't hear that door open without starting. Hell! ... Bring me another cocktail, waiter."

"Steady, old chap! Your nerves are dicky, that's what's the matter with you."

"It's the first time in my life," Harvey Grimm muttered, "but I've got them now. I feel that I'm cornered. I did Brodie in this morning. I left him at eleven o'clock, gagged and tied in the workshop he tracked me to. I was Edward Levy there, and there isn't one of them except the old man who knew otherwise. Brodie himself never recognised me. The only fear is if the old man peaches. He's had a couple of thousand of the best, and he hoards gold and loves it as though it were his own lifeblood. Thank God, here are the cocktails!"

"I shall write an epic about you this afternoon," the poet declared. "You're tense, Harvey, that's what you are. You're strung up. There's a different sense in the words you speak, a sort of quivering significance in everything you say. You're feeling life, man."

"I'm feeling afraid, if that's anything," Harvey Grimm confessed, raising his glass. "There was a woman in it, of course—and God knows I was careful!—a fierce, strong young Jewess. If she gets her grandfather by the throat, she'll wring the truth out of him."

Cresswell rose to his feet.

"It will do you good to eat, my friend," he suggested. "I find you exciting, vibrating, stimulating, but you are wearing yourself out."

Harvey Grimm sat with tightly clenched fists.

"I'm afraid to go in the restaurant," he said. "Do you notice how that man at the bar is staring, Cresswell? Who's he?"

"Don't be a silly ass!" his companion exclaimed. "That's Greaves, the London correspondent of the *New York Trombone*. He'd be all over our story if he knew it. Come along. Pull yourself together, man … upright!"

Harvey Grimm did his best. He walked into the restaurant with almost his usual airy *bonhomie*. An acquaintance stopped the two men.

"Wouldn't look at me in Fitz's, Grimm," he complained. "Getting proud, old chap?"

"Sorry," Harvey Grimm replied. "I saw your back afterwards. I was looking at a man over your shoulder."

They seated themselves at their usual table. Another chance acquaintance paused to speak to them.

"Thought you'd given up this place, Grimm. Saw you at the Piccadilly on Thursday."

"I like a change sometimes," the latter observed. "How's the new play going?"

"Capitally, thanks!"

The actor passed on. Harvey Grimm glanced at a sheet of paper which he brought out from his pocket.

"Yes," he murmured, "I was at the Piccadilly on Thursday. Nothing like being thorough in these things, Stephen. My alibi was pretty successful, eh?"

"Mean to say you get a chap to go about when you're in hiding, and establish alibis for you?" the poet asked wonderingly.

"That's exactly the idea," Harvey Grimm agreed, "and to tell you the truth, if I hadn't a fit of nerves on me I should say that my alibis would take a little upsetting."

They ordered luncheon and a bottle of wine, but for some reason or other the old spirit was lacking. They missed Aaron Rodd and speculated as to the cause of his absence. Cresswell, too, seemed to have inherited a new seriousness with his unaccustomed attire. It was their mutual recognition of the drawing to an end of one little cycle of their life, and try though he might, Harvey Grimm could never escape from the queer sense of foreboding which had haunted him for the last few hours. And then, towards the end of the meal, a page-boy came into the room, gazed around for a moment and approached their table.

"Two gentlemen would like to speak to you, Mr. Grimm," he announced.

Harvey Grimm laid down his knife and fork. He nodded to the boy, but there was a queer, hunted look in his eyes as he turned towards his companion.

"Stephen, old fellow," he muttered, "it's come."

The poet laid his hand upon his friend's shoulder.

"Look here, Harvey," he asked, "do you want to make a scrap of it? I'm your man, if you do. Or I say, have you anything you'd like to hand over to me? I can stand the racket."

Harvey Grimm shook his head firmly.

"No," he decided, "if it's the end, well, I'll face it. If only Jerry hadn't cleared out I might have got rid of the stones. Good-bye, Stephen, and good luck to you! Better follow me out, perhaps, if I don't return."

He made his way without undue haste from the room, exchanging one or two greetings, pausing, even, in the swing doors to say a few words with a friend. Then, when he stood in the little lobby, he knew that there was truth at the back of all his forebodings. It was a well-known Scotland Yard inspector and a subordinate, both in plain clothes, who were standing there with their hats in their hands. The inspector greeted him cheerily, but dropped his voice.

"Mr. Grimm," he said, "I'll have to trouble you to come along to headquarters. Just a few questions, you understand—as quietly as you like. You see, we've come here in mufti. Go back and say good-bye to your friend, if you want to."

"That's very considerate of you, Inspector," was the grateful reply. "I'll just tap the window, if you'll allow me."

The poet obeyed the summons promptly. Harvey Grimm met him by the door and took his arm.

"They're after me, Stephen," he confided. "They're doing it jolly civilly, though. There's a time for going on to the bitter end and there's a time for dropping it. I'm dropping it. Once more, good luck to you!"

The two men gripped hands. The page-boy came up again and touched Harvey Grimm on the shoulder.

"Wanted on the telephone, sir," he announced.

The former turned towards the inspector.

"Pray, don't hurry, Mr. Grimm," the latter remarked courteously. "Our time is entirely yours."

Harvey Grimm stepped into the telephone box and took up the receiver. The voice that answered his enquiry was hoarse, as though with some unnatural emotion.

"Is that Harvey Grimm?"

"Yes!"

"This is Aaron—Aaron Rodd. Where are you? Can you come and help? I'm in trouble."

"So am I," Harvey Grimm replied, a little bitterly. "What's yours?"

"I came down to Tilbury this morning with Henriette, to see her brother off. We couldn't find him. Henriette got on the wrong steamer and they've taken her off. It was a trap, Harvey, do you hear? They've got her!"

"Where are you?"

"I'm at Tilbury, telephoning from the docks," was the hoarse reply. "The whole thing was a sell. The munition boat by which Brinnen was supposed to leave has never been heard of. Can you come down?"

Harvey Grimm closed the door tightly behind him and almost whispered down the telephone.

"Can you hear, Aaron?"

"Yes!"

"Jerry Sands has got away all right. He wasn't on any munition boat! I was arrested five minutes ago. I'm being taken to Scotland Yard, and I've fifty thousand pounds' worth of his diamonds on me! I shouldn't worry about the girl if I were you, Aaron. I think Jerry Sands' sister can take care of herself!"

"Where's Cresswell?"

"Here with me."

"Could he come?"

"He's joined an O.T.C. I don't suppose he could get leave. Besides, can't you understand, Aaron? She is Jerry Sands' sister and they're off together somewhere, for certain.... What's that? ... What? ..."

There was a confused babel of sounds—nothing more distinct. The connection had been cut. Harvey Grimm spent five minutes in vain, trying to re-establish it. Then he left the booth.

"Nice cropper for us, Stephen," he announced to the poet, who was waiting outside. "That was Aaron. The girl's given him the slip down at Tilbury. He's like a madman, of course."

The inspector, who had lit his second cigarette, strolled up.

"I am afraid," he said, "that people are beginning to recognise us. Don't you think—?"

"You are quite right, sir," Harvey Grimm assented. "You have been very considerate. I am entirely at your service now. Good luck to you, Cresswell. Go back and finish your luncheon. You can sign the bill for me."

The poet played the game and departed, after a hearty handshake. Harvey Grimm took his seat in a taxicab, the inspector by his side, the constable opposite. They drove off.

"Enquiries, eh?" Harvey Grimm ruminated. "I wonder what you want to enquire about?"

"I fancy," the inspector said confidentially, "that the Chief will start by having you searched."

"What do you expect to find, if it's a fair question?"

The inspector smiled. He had thrust his arm in friendly fashion through his companion's.

"We've an idea," he replied, "that this time we shall find a few of Jerry Sands' diamonds."

CHAPTER X

THE END OF JEREMIAH SANDS

Aaron Rodd clasped his arms a little further around the barrel against which he was leaning, trod water with his feet and thought about death. The curtain of a slight mist had fallen around him. There was nothing visible but the cold, grey sea, sometimes high above his head, sometimes like a water-slide tumbling away many feet below him. All around him he could hear the hooting of the steamers, sounding their weird notes of warning from some unseen, unimaginable world. A few feet away, also clinging to a barrel, was a bronzed and hairy man in nautical attire, who was using the most awful language.

"No good wasting your breath," Aaron gasped. "Try another shout."

The man did as he was advised, without eliciting any reply from the other side of the grey walls, whereupon he proceeded once more, in lurid language, to express his opinion of murdering foreigners, and mysterious gents who tempted honest tug-masters into doubtful enterprises. Suddenly he broke off.

"Crikey! 'Ere's something on the top of us!" he exclaimed. "Shout, guv'nor, quick!"

Once more Aaron Rodd drew a long breath and shouted. His voice sounded like a child's falsetto, lost in the stentorian roar of his companion's demand for immediate help and rescue. Then the grey fog was suddenly pierced. A huge, dark mass seemed to be gliding almost on the top of them. From somewhere up in the clouds came an answering shout. Aaron Rodd's companion was moved to one supreme and successful effort. A clear, loud voice shouted directions to them.

"We're lowering ropes. Catch hold, if you can, before the wash. We'll lower boats in a minute."

Half a dozen ropes came down like curving snakes. One of them hit the water scarcely a foot from Aaron. He gripped it tightly.

"Twist it round your body, mate," his companion spluttered. "Twist it two or three times round and hold on for dear life."

The next few minutes were barely realisable. Aaron felt himself tossed like a cork on to the top of a seething mass of churned-up sea, flung down again with the roar of it in his cars, left for a moment in peace and then dragged through the water at such a pace that he found himself wondering whether his arms were going to be torn from his body. Then he was shot forward with a new impetus. His body and arms ached with the strain. He was only half conscious.

"That's done it, matey," he heard his companion shout. "Hold on, there's the boat coming."

Aaron Rodd never wholly lost consciousness. He heard the measured beat of the oars, the sharp, clear voice of the officer standing up in the stern. He saw the boat emerge from the gloom, heard the quick orders, felt himself lifted up by the shoulders, felt the luxury of something solid beneath his feet. The officer in charge of the boat looked at the two men curiously.

"What's this?" he asked. "Collision?"

Aaron Rodd's companion took a long breath and tried to explain what it was. The officer listened to him, spellbound. The men almost forgot to row.

"Some one seems to have been playing a dirty trick on you, eh?" the former remarked, when at last the mariner ceased through sheer exhaustion. "Well, you can tell the Commander when we get on board."

Gradually a fuller consciousness returned to Aaron Rodd. He was able to walk along the deck of the ship they boarded, to grope his way, unaided, down the narrow stairs into the small cabin below, where a man was seated at a table with a chart before him. He pushed it away as the two men were ushered in.

"Hullo, what's this?" he exclaimed.

The officer who had brought them made a brief report. The Commander nodded.

"Fetch them some hot whisky, quick," he directed. "Now tell us your story."

The tug-master got in first, but after a few sentences the Commander stopped him.

"I think I'll get at the truth quicker from you," he decided, nodding to Aaron. "Quick, please."

Aaron pulled himself together and took a long gulp of the hot whisky which was 'at that moment brought in.

"May I enquire if this is an English man-of-war?" he asked, as he set the glass down.

"His Majesty's destroyer, *Flying Fox*," was the brief reply. "Now tell me what you two men are doing on barrels in the North Sea?"

Aaron Rodd found a few terse and explicit words.

"Early this morning," he said, "I escorted a young lady to Tilbury. We went there on the strength of a bogus telegram, which informed us that her brother, who is a Belgian officer, was leaving there at midday on a munition ship bound for Havre. We found a ship's boat waiting for us at the dock mentioned in the telegram, but they refused to take me on board with her. I thought this reasonable, as it was supposed to be a Government vessel, and I stayed behind to wait for her. She was no sooner safely on board than the steamer hoisted the Norwegian flag and steamed off."

The Commander stared for a moment. Then he looked away.

"Sounds a queer story," he observed.

"It's a true one," Aaron assured him. "Of course, there's a reason for this abduction. The young lady some months ago—"

"I don't want the whole story," the Commander interrupted. "I want to know how you got into the North Sea?"

"I was coming to that," Aaron Rodd proceeded. "My companion can bear me out as to the rest. I hired his tug, meaning to follow the steamer into whatever port it might go if they refused to take me on board. We caught her up and signalled her to stop. She manoeuvred a little, disclosed a gun, and blew us to pieces. The captain here and I are the only two who ever came up again."

The Commander glanced at the lieutenant, who had remained in the room. Not a word passed between them.

"Who are you?" he enquired.

"My name is Aaron Rodd," was the prompt reply. "I am an American, but I have practised law in England for a good many years. I know my story sounds fanciful, but there's no getting away from the sequel. The tug-master here can confirm every word of it."

The tug-master proceeded to do so, and the two officers listened for a time as though fascinated. The Commander interrupted him at last.

"What's the name of this boat?" he asked.

"She had S.S. *Christiania* painted across her stern," the tug-master said, "and she was flying the Norwegian flag, but the ship's name's new painted. I passed close alongside yesterday, and a queer-looking lot they were on board."

The two officers exchanged quick glances.

"The *Christiania*," the Commander murmured softly.

He paused for a moment and bent over the chart. Then he looked up.

"Take Mr. Rodd and the tug-master to the ward-room," he directed. "Rig them both out in some dry clothes and see that they have everything they want."

Aaron Rodd had forgotten the discomfort of his condition. He had only one idea in his brain.

"Sir," he told the Commander, "that ship, the *Christiania*, is in the pay of the Germans."

"You may be right, Mr. Rodd," the latter assented. "When you have changed your clothes, come down and have another chat, if I am not on the bridge."

Even then Aaron lingered.

"Sir," he went on, "I know that there's nothing I can say will keep you for one moment from what you think to be your duty. I have just had a fortune left me in America. I'll give a destroyer to the British Navy if you'll overhaul the *Christiania*, search her, and take that young lady off."

The Commander smiled.

"The British Navy doesn't need bribing, sir," he said. "I've had a hint about the *Christiania* myself. I'll see what can be done. Now off you go and get into those dry clothes."

The two unexpected guests were hospitably entertained in the wardroom, and Aaron Rodd made a very creditable appearance, an hour later, in some oddments of naval uniform. They found their way on deck, but were only allowed at the top of the companionway. The fog had lifted. There were half a dozen steamers in sight, and the destroyer seemed to be completing a rather violent curve. Suddenly there were loud orders. The roar of the machinery was lessened. She glided through the water, slackening speed at every instant. Looking down the deck they could see a sight which thrilled them both. The tug-master understood it better than Aaron.

"She's cleared for action, guv'nor!" he exclaimed. "The gunners are all at their posts. See the signal. My God, that's the *Christiania*!"

He pointed to the steamer round which they had circled.

"They've signalled her to stop," he continued. "If I get my hands on the captain! ... Hullo, another signal! Watch it, guv'nor. That's the last call—' Heave to at once or'—"

"Or what?" Aaron Rodd asked.

The tug-master smacked his lips.

"Those little six-inch boys will talk," he replied, with gusto. "We could send the *Christiania* to the bottom in something less than thirty seconds. You watch the angle of those guns. Look at the man's face who's just had an order! He's trained on her.... My God!"

The *Christiania* had pursued her course. Suddenly there was a deafening roar, a vibration which shook the ship. Fifty yards in front of the *Christiania* the sea was all churned into foam.

"It's just an 'int!" the tug-master exclaimed in delight. "It's a blankety 'int! Look at 'em running about on board."

There were signs of an immense commotion on board the *Christiania*. Another signal slowly fluttered to the masthead. The tug-master, who was watching the steamer's progress, grinned.

"They're giving in," he declared. "They've stopped the engines. Oh, if they'd only let me go on board her!"

The lieutenant came running lightly down the bridge and approached Aaron.

"We are sending a crew on board the *Christiania*," he announced. "You'd better go and see if you can identify the young lady. There's a boat being lowered from the other deck."

"May I go along, sir?" the tug-master asked eagerly.

The officer shook his head.

"You stay where you are, my man," he directed. "You'll get compensation for your tug, if your story turns out to be true."

The man sighed.

"There's two sorts of compensation," he muttered, as he spat upon his hands.

Aaron Rodd sat by the side of the lieutenant, and though he had never done such a thing in his life before, he stepped confidently up the rope ladder after him and boarded the *Christiania*. The captain was waiting to receive them. He was a small, very fair man, who spoke English with a harsh and guttural accent. His manner was exceedingly perturbed.

"By what right, will you tell me, this piracy?" he demanded, barely accepting the lieutenant's salute. "My papers were cleared in London. My cargo—"

"A few words with you below, if you please, Captain," the lieutenant interrupted. "You had better stay on deck, Mr. Rodd," he added, looking around.

Aaron walked up and down and endeavoured unsuccessfully to converse with various members of the crew. The ship bore all the usual evidences of being a small cargo steamer, but there was, to his fancy, something sinister in the appearance of the sailors and the sound of their conversation as they pointed to the destroyer—long, grey and evil-looking, rising and falling upon the waves, a short distance away. Suddenly a man who might have been a steward appeared from below and touched him on the shoulder.

"Come this way, please," he invited.

He led Aaron downstairs into a dark, odoriferous saloon. The captain and the English lieutenant were seated at the top of one of the long tables. The latter motioned Aaron Rodd to approach.

"The captain denies having any passenger on board, Mr. Rodd," he observed.

"I saw a young lady taken on board at Tilbury," Aaron pronounced firmly. "She was brought here under a false pretext, and she is here now."

"It is not true," the captain declared furiously. "There is no young lady on board."

"What do you say to that, Mr. Rodd?" the lieutenant enquired.

Aaron leaned a little forward. He stretched out his hand, and the captain for a moment shrank back.

"The man is lying," he said calmly. "The young lady was brought here under the pretext of seeing her brother. If this vessel is allowed to proceed on its way to Norway she will be intercepted somewhere by a German boat, and the young lady will be made a prisoner. That is a certainty."

"The gentleman has made a mistake," the captain insisted. "There were many vessels lying in the Thames yesterday morning. We do not carry passengers."

The boatswain of the destroyer, who had accompanied them on board, entered the saloon and, coming up to the lieutenant, saluted.

"Could I have a word with you, sir?" he asked.

The lieutenant rose to his feet and retired for a few moments to the further end of the saloon. When he returned, his manner had undergone a change.

"Captain Hooge," he said, "in confirmation of this gentleman's story I find that you have two concealed guns on board, and there are other suspicious circumstances which my boatswain has pointed out, which confirm my own impressions about you. I am signalling for a prize crew and shall take you to Harwich."

The captain sprang to his feet. His eyes were red with fury.

"You damned, meddlesome Englishmen!" he cried. "If you keep me here another hour, you will hear of it! My Government will protest. It is contrary to the accepted principles of maritime law."

"It is very much against the principles of maritime law, as I read it," the lieutenant answered coolly, "for you to blow to pieces, with a concealed gun, a tug which simply came up to ask you questions. Now be a sensible man, Captain Hooge. I shall have your ship searched from top to bottom. If the young lady is found, you will have to stand your trial in an English court on an extremely serious charge."

"If there is any young lady on board," the captain declared sullenly, "it is without my knowledge. I will go and see the purser."

"We will come, too," the lieutenant said dryly.

They passed down a little companionway.

The captain opened the door of a small stateroom and talked for some time in Norwegian to a bearded and spectacled man. The latter, after some time, turned towards the two men and spoke in English.

"There is a young lady here. She must have boarded us by accident. We were on the point of starting, and we could not land her. Come this way."

They followed the man down a long gloomy passage. He knocked at the door of a stateroom at the end of it. A faint voice answered. The door was thrown open. Henriette, white and eager, stood shrinking back against the wall. There was a rush of cold air into the place.

"Aaron!" she exclaimed in blank astonishment. "Aaron Rodd!"

Words failed her altogether. It seemed too wonderful. She peered into his face, shook him by the shoulders, and finally almost collapsed in his arms.

"It's all right, Henriette," he cried, his own voice shaking. "You're quite safe."

"But where did you come from? How did you get here?" she gasped.

"I followed in a tug," he told her. "These pleasant people blew us up."

"I heard the gun!" she cried. "I saw the tug. I saw it go down! I saw the men swimming in the water. It was horrible."

"I was one of them," Aaron continued. "The master and I were picked up by an English destroyer. This is one of the officers. I managed to make them believe my story and we overhauled and boarded your steamer. We are going to take it into Harwich. You are safe, Henriette."

She began to sob. The tears stood in Aaron's own eyes as he saw thrust through the open porthole the umbrella on which she had tied various fragments of clothing.

"I have been waving this out of the porthole," she explained hysterically. "I thought they might see. I was locked in until a moment ago."

"Better bring the young lady up on deck," the officer suggested. "We've no accommodation for you on board the *Flying Fox*, but I am going to signal the Commander for a prize crew, and place the captain and officers of this ship under arrest, so you'll both feel quite safe here. You'll be in Harwich in five hours and we shall be standing by all the time."

"You won't leave me, Aaron?" she begged.

"Not I!" he answered heartily.

"I expect I shall take the steamer in," the officer remarked. "You are quite safe now, young lady," he added reassuringly. "I should come on deck and get a little fresh air, if I were you."

She clung to Aaron as they passed out. They met the captain and the purser talking together in the companionway. The former saluted a little awkwardly.

"Sorry to hear that there was a mistake, miss," he said. "We were expecting a young lady on board, the daughter of the owner, who had been giving her people some trouble."

Henriette simply looked at the man. He turned away.

"I want to go on deck," she whispered to Aaron. "I want to get away from this atmosphere. Come quickly, please.... Oh, look, look!"

Half a dozen English sailors came down the companionway. They were in war trim and they looked like ruddy goliaths by the side of the pale, anaemic-looking crew of the *Christiania*. Henriette gave a little sob.

"I feel safe," she cried, "safe, after all.... Aaron!"

"Yes, dear?"

Her little face, so white and pitiful, was strained up to his. The ghost of one of her old provocative smiles quivered at her lips.

"Even Leopold," she murmured, "will not be able to say 'no' any longer. Do you know that you are a wonderful person? You are like one of those heroes in romances. There never was such a rescue."

He pressed her arm.

"Our last adventure," he whispered, "is going to be the greatest of all."

* * * *

The magistrate's court was crowded almost to suffocation when for the third time Harvey Grimm was charged with having aided and abetted in the theft of various jewels found in his possession. The solicitor for the Treasury rose at once when called upon, urbane, even apologetic, yet firm.

"I trust that this time, Mr. Dyson," the magistrate remarked, "you are in a position to offer sufficient evidence to enable me either to discharge or to send the prisoner for trial?"

The solicitor for the Treasury proceeded to explain. He reminded their Worships that the prisoner had been discovered last week, owing to the assiduous efforts of Mr. Brodie, actually engaged in secretly cutting up and disguising valuable diamonds. There was no question at all but that these diamonds were stolen. The trouble which the prosecution had to contend with was the fact that they were stolen in America, and that some of the stones had been mutilated in such a fashion as to render them almost unrecognisable. A commission from the police force of New York had already sailed, not only to identify the jewels, but with a strong hope of identifying the prisoner as a confederate of one of the most notorious jewel thieves of this generation. He was exceedingly sorry to have to ask for a fourth remand, but in this case there was no alternative.

He sat down. A mild-mannered man arose from his side and addressed the magistrate.

"Your Worship," he said, "I am defending the prisoner. In the event of the prosecution having no further evidence to offer today, which I understand to be the case, may I be allowed to call a witness?" The magistrate coughed.

"You would be within your rights, Mr. Hansome," he admitted, leaning forward and looking over his eyeglasses, "but I need scarcely remind you that, to a certain extent, by calling witnesses for the defence at this stage of the proceedings you might possibly prejudice your client's case."

The solicitor bowed.

"My client being a wholly innocent man, your Worship," he said, "is only anxious to have the truth known as soon as possible."

"You can do as you choose, Mr. Hansome," the magistrate consented.

There was a moment's whispering. A name only partially heard was called outside, and a ripple of interest passed through the court when Captain Brinnen, still in his Belgian uniform, entered the witness-box. The solicitor for the prosecution looked a little staggered. The solicitor for the defence stood up.

"Will you tell the magistrate your name?" he asked.

The witness bowed.

"Leopold Francis Henri Brinnen dc Floge."

"And your titles?"

"Comte de Malaison, Baron d'Asche, Chevalier di Scolo, Vicomte de Floge."

There was a distinct sensation in court, a sense of impending events which left every one pleasantly excited. Harvey Grimm leaned forward, gripping at the rail in front of him.

"You are, I believe," the solicitor continued, "a godson of the late King of the Belgians?"

"That is so," the witness admitted.

"Do you know anything of the prisoner?"

The witness glanced at Harvey Grimm and, meeting his astounded stare, greeted him in friendly fashion.

"Certainly," he replied. "Mr. Harvey Grimm is a valued acquaintance. I engaged him recently to re-cut and, if possible, to present to me in an altered form a variety of precious stones."

"May I ask your reason for this?" the solicitor enquired.

"It is a matter of almost political history," the witness explained, turning towards the magistrate. "The De Floge collection of diamonds is famous, I believe I may say, throughout the world. They were the subject, at the time of the outbreak of the war, of a lawsuit between the German branch of the De Floge family and my own. During the hearing of the case, the jewels were deposited by common consent at the Antwerp Museum, where anybody who is an expert in these matters will tell you that they have been inspected by connoisseurs from all over the world. With the invasion of our country, my grandfather and I determined to do our best to prevent these jewels, which were worth an immense sum, from falling into the hands of the enemy. The curators of the Antwerp Museum, although they were under a bond, consented, under the circumstances, to hand them over to our branch of the family, and they were transported to my grandfather's château, which is very near the French frontier, just before the sack of Antwerp. Subsequently my grandfather and my sister, the Comtesse de Floge, after a series of remarkable adventures, in which the latter especially was concerned, managed to escape to England with the bulk of the jewels. My cousin, however, who represents the German side of our family, has seized our lands and home and has made desperate attempts in various directions to secure also the jewels, which the authorities would now award him as a matter of course. I deemed it wise, bearing all these things in mind, to yield to my grandfather's almost passionate insistence and dispose secretly of as many as possible."

There was a great sensation in court. Mr. Harvey Grimm asked for a chair and sat down.

"Did you," the solicitor for the defence asked, "impose entire secrecy upon Mr. Harvey Grimm?"

"Under the peculiar circumstances of the case, I did," was the prompt reply.

The solicitor turned to the magistrate.

"There is nothing left, your Worship," he said, "but for me to ask you to sanction the immediate release of my client."

He resumed his seat. The solicitor for the prosecution promptly arose.

"I may be allowed, your Worship," he asked, "to cross-examine the witness?"

"Certainly," the magistrate assented.

"May I ask you, sir, whether you have any evidence in support of these extraordinary statements of yours?"

The young man bowed.

"Certainly," he replied. "The Belgian Minister, who was my father's greatest friend and relative, and the Princess Augusta, my godmother, are both, I believe, present."

The solicitor for the prosecution turned to the magistrate.

"If these witnesses may be called and are found to support the story, your Worship," he said, "the case for the prosecution is withdrawn."

Leopold de Floge left the witness-box, strolled along the back of the benches, and held out his hand to Harvey Grimm.

"My profound regrets and apologies," he murmured. "I wait here and we will lunch together."

The court rocked itself with excitement. The Belgian Minister was called and promptly took his place in the witness-box. Asked if he knew the last witness, his reply was comprehensive.

"The Vicomte de Floge," he said, "is the first nobleman in Belgium. He is a godson of the late king, is himself connected with the royal family, and is a young man whose gallantry in the field has won special commendation from the King."

"Do you know anything about the De Floge diamonds?"

"Certainly," the witness replied. "They are of historical and priceless value, and special efforts were made to seize them at Antwerp Museum. My friend, the Vicomte de Floge, was able to rescue them just in time. I may say that he consulted me, and under the difficult circumstances I advised him to dispose of as many as possible secretly. Very powerful influences have been brought to bear through a neutral country, to effect their restoration."

The magistrate bowed and the witness stood down. There was a moment's whispered consultation between the two solicitors. Then one of them stood up.

"The case for the prosecution is withdrawn, your Worship," he announced.

Harvey Grimm and Leopold de Floge, by the courtesy of the magistrate, left the court by the back entrance, arm in arm. The former was looking a little haggard from his six days' detention, and was scarcely his usual spick-and-span self. He was a little dazed, too. He leaned back in a luxurious motorcar and tried to realise what had happened. His first question was not an unnatural one.

"Will you tell me," he asked earnestly, "why your grandfather, and you, and your sister, all practically confessed that you were Jeremiah Sands, the international jewel thief?"

"I must admit that the idea was my own," De Floge explained. "You see, we were extremely anxious that no one should know whose jewels these really were. The one way to ensure absolute secrecy was to dispose of them as stolen property. That is what we did, and I must say that under the circumstances, Mr. Grimm, your silence was more than admirable. To a great extent, I must admit, we were humouring my grandfather, who was oppressed the whole of the time with a nervous fear of being ordered by the British Government to restore them. His death makes all the difference—in fact, I have this morning entrusted the whole of the rest of my collection to Christie's, and they will offer them for sale as soon as the South American buyers can be duly advised. It is, perhaps, just as well that we have passed the crisis, for I see by this morning's papers that Jeremiah Sands was arrested at Chicago yesterday."

Harvey Grimm cleared his throat.

"You haven't such a thing as a cigarette, I suppose?"

De Floge produced his case at once.

"My profound apologies," he said. "I should have known the one thing you needed most after this regrettable detention."

"To think," Harvey Grimm muttered to himself, "that I stole way down to Letchowiski's and lived in terror of my life, with that rat of a Brodie dogging my footsteps, and all the time I might have fitted up a laboratory and have done my work at home!"

"That would never have done," De Floge objected. "By the decision of the Belgian courts—German-inspired, of course, but still according to the law of the land—the whole of the jewels are, in a way, stolen property. Still—it is not the sort of theft that counts."

Harvey Grimm looked out of the windows. There was a queer sort of plaintive happiness dawning in his face.

"It's London all right," he murmured, "the Strand, too. ... I never thought to see them again—not till I was an old man, at any rate. Where are we going?"

"The Milan for luncheon," De Floge replied, "where you will meet some friends. I have more wonders to tell you. Will you hear them first or wait till you have had a cocktail?"

"More wonders," Harvey Grimm murmured, "and this is the city which lacks the spirit of adventure! I think," he went on, as they stepped out of the car and walked towards the smoke-room, "you must leave this to me. There is just one concoction—I can't call it by a name. I must speak to Coley. What a cigarette!" he went on. "For six days—"

"I know," De Floge interrupted. "I am sorry. We will try and make up for it."

They drank a cocktail together, and the sense of unreality began to fall away. Once more the earth was firm beneath Harvey Grimm's feet.

"The money I have wasted!" he groaned. "Why, I had a young actor establishing alibis for me all the time I was away! ... Where's Aaron?"

"Just back from the North Sea with my sister," De Floge replied. "He will tell you a story that will make your hair stand on end."

"And the poet?"

"Down with an Officers' Training Corps. He is coming up to lunch, if he can get off."

Harvey Grimm glanced at the clock. His companion interpreted his thoughts.

"You have an hour," he said.

"A shave and a bath," the other murmured ecstatically.

"And the corner table as you come in, in the grill-room," De Floge added. "We will all meet there at one-thirty...."

Some time before the hour had elapsed Harvey Grimm was entirely his usual self. Shaved and bathed, clad in one of his favourite blue serge suits, patent shoes and spotless gaiters, a bunch of violets in his buttonhole, a sense of stupefied but immeasurable satisfaction radiating from him, he took his place at the round luncheon table, between Aaron Rodd and Henriette, and raised the glass of amber liquid which he found waiting there, to his lips. De Floge, however, checked him.

"My friends," he said, "but wait. Here is Mr. Cresswell."

The poet came to them with outstretched hands.

"My heartiest congratulations!" he exclaimed, pausing before Harvey Grimm. "You will be able to write a ballad of the Bow Street cells. Perhaps I will collaborate. It will mean immortality for you. Where do I sit?"

A place was found for him. He, too, raised the wine-glass which he found in front of him, to his lips, but was checked by De Floge.

"We will, with your permission," the latter proposed, "drink to the happiness of my dear sister, Henriette, and your friend—and mine, too, that is to be," he added, with a bow—"Mr. Aaron Rodd. They are to be married this month, and if you would care for a wonderful entertainment during the service of our luncheon, they shall recount their adventures of the last six days. I promise you, Mr. Harvey Grimm, that yours will seem to you monotonous."

They listened to the story, told by one and supplemented by the other. It was all amazing. The poet was frankly envious.

"After all," he grumbled, "it seems to me that I am the one who treads the dreary path of commonplace life."

De Floge leaned across towards him.

"Sir," he said, "that is not wholly true, for both you and I, along different paths, are pledged to the greatest and most wonderful adventure the world can offer. We have drunk to the happiness of my sister and Mr. Aaron Rodd. I drank to you a short while ago, Mr. Harvey Grimm, full of respect for that sporting spirit which kept you silent in captivity. We will drink now, all of us, to the common cause, to the great adventure of life and death, to the end which is written in letters of blood across the scarred face of Europe—to Vengeance and Victory!"